THE DARKLAND WAR:
CENTAUR'S RETURN.

By Stacey Erin Welsh.

The Darkland War: Centaur's Return

© 2014 Stacey Welsh

This book is a work of fiction. Any similarities to persons, locations or events is purely coincidental and unintentional.

This book is protected by international copyright laws.

First printed 2017.

Edited by: Susan Horsnell.

Published by SJR Independent/Far Horizons Publishing.

ISBN-10:0-6480098-4-X

ISBN-13:978-0-6480098-4-9

For more information about the author, new releases and news, follow or Like Stacey Welsh on Facebook:

www.facebook.com/staceywelshauthor/

Prologue:

Deep into the southern lands they had come, slaying, enslaving and burning whoever and whatever they had come across. There was no warning, and no reason for Beru, the Centaur king, to rain death and destruction on the peoples of the Southern Lands.

Together with his Orcish allies, he had forced his way through the borders with Belline, Erellond, Vallonde and the Iron Kingdom, homelands of Man, Elf and Dwarf.

Now, after a year of bloody war at the great cost of life and land, the allied armies of the South had pushed back the Centaur war host to a valley where they barely managed to hold their enemy.

Every day, they lost ground and regained it in battle, but their stalemate could not hold out forever. The loss of soldiers on both sides was constant, but with less chance of replenishment for the Southern allies, their hopes for victory were fading.

In desperation, the allied kings of the south gathered together their greatest wizards and magicians, and fashioned a spell, for if they could not defeat their enemy, they would have no choice but to surrender. The spell had been fashioned at great cost to the lives of the magicians, and wizards, and at its casting, much of the magic of the world would be depleted.

Thousands of Wizards and mages had died to stop the Darkland forces through their arcane arts, a sacrifice they hoped would not be in vain.

***

Beru stood watching as the Southern host gathered in their war camps across the battlefield, watching and waiting. His own great armies were ready for their final onslaught, and this time they would break through, cutting down the pathetic fools that stood against him. Their deaths would be more the sweeter for him and the enslavement of the people of the southern kingdoms of Man, Elf and Dwarf would follow swiftly.

His lip curled in a sneer as he gazed over the Southerner's ragged forward lines as they formed up, the nervous energy as the younger soldiers faced death was rife in the air.

"Prepare the charge." He said to his Orcish general.

"At once, my Lord." The Orc, clad in heavy battle armour nodded. He turned and roared orders to his lackeys as he strode away to his men. Each Orc and Centaur under the command of the Orc snapped to attention and moved to their places, readying themselves for the bloody charge.

Beru heard the clinking of weapons and armour as his own men prepared themselves, the clattering of hoof on stone, muffled by the mass of warm bodies and the quiet muttering of troops as they prayed to the war gods for a glorious victory in the coming battle.

Beru turned to look and saw his men were ready to attack. He turned and scanned the enemy lines, they were still getting into position.

He drew his sword from its scabbard and roared, pointing the sharp end of the blade at the enemy lines. His powerful equine body surged forward as his army moved as one behind him.

***

Across the battlefield, the allied armies of the Southern Kingdoms saw the oncoming enemy. A scout ran towards the pavilion of the Southern Kings

"My Lords!" he said, gasping for breath. "The enemy has begun the charge!"

King Aderon, the Elven king of Erellond looked up from the map table, the slight arch to his eyebrows the only sign of his shock and surprise that their enemy were ready with such speed.

"We have no more time. Summon the wizards, hold them off for as long as we can, it ends here and now." He said as he turned to the other kings. "May we see this day through, my brother Kings." He said and bowed his head.

"Let what follows be our finest hour." King Helven of the Iron Kingdom said, he downed the last mug of warm ale on the table before nodding and holding his hand out to each of his fellow kings to shake his small, but strong dwarven hand.

"We all know what must be done, let us not falter from our paths, let us brave this day like we have each day before." King Var of Vallonde nodded as he strapped his helm to his head, his squire buckling it tight and handing him his sword.

"My lords, let this be a day of glory for all." King Keron said as he nodded to the others, he turned and strode with purpose from the pavilion, his own squire following him with an armful of weapons and armour.

King Aderon turned to the door flap of the pavilion as the last few surviving magicians and wizards arrived and bowed to the assembled kings.

"My lord mages, it is time and now the hour of truth is upon us, I hope that your spell is prepared."

"Yes, my King." One of the Elven wizards nodded, "We need but one final thing from each of you. A drop of royal blood." The Magician said as he bowed. He held out a crystal and a dagger.

King Aderon took the dagger and pierced his finger, a tiny drop of crimson blood flowed to the end of his finger where he had pricked it. Then he pressed his finger onto the crystal. As the stone turned a soft pink colour, a magician fell to the earth with a cry. His life forces chained to the Crystal, it sucked the life from his body as it generated the power from the spell. Aderon looked shocked, but the master wizard nodded for him to continue.

"It is our sacrifice to the cause, my king. We do this humbly, for our wives and children may survive this day whereas we may not."

The Elven King was silent as he handed the dagger to the next king, Helven followed Aderon's example as did Var. The crystal was now a bright red in the hands of the wizard who now stood with one wizard left, two more wizards fallen with the blood sacrifice to the crystal.

"My Lord, we still need the last king's blood, else the crystal will fail and the spell will be miscast!" The magician said as the sounds of battle grew to a roar outside the pavilion.

"He is engaged in battle already! We must get to him." Aderon said as he turned to his brother kings. He gathered his weapons and strode out to join the battle, the other kings and the magicians following.

"Should he fall and we fail, all will be lost." The Magician said as they ran to the battle

***

The smell of blood, dust and fear flowed through Beru's nose as he raised his sword and struck hard into the shoulder of a human soldier, The metal of his sword parted the weak leather of the man's armour and a spurt of blood fountained from a severed artery as the man screamed and fell, clutching a gauntleted hand at his neck.

Beru trampled over him, his soft warm body crushed under the Centaur King's sharp hooves and heavy weight.

9

His bloodlust burned hot through his veins as he sought out another enemy soldier to slay.

"Beru! Come meet your fate at the end of my blade!" a voice made bold by rage and adrenalin carried to his ears. Beru looked to his left and saw one of the kings of Men standing there in armour splattered in purple orc blood.

"Ah... Keron the Great, at last I meet you on the battlefield. Did you know, your son Bedeon begged for my mercy when I met him a few months ago, Needless to say, I am not merciful to fools. I wonder if he learned his begging skills from you..." the Centaur king drew his bloodied blade across his tongue to clean it, preparing the steel to taste the blood of a royal. "Let us see, shall we?" he said as he surged forward, bringing his body to charge the enemy king before him.

Keron prepared himself as best one could against the charging Centaur. He dodged the blade, a slight nick to his skin causing a pearl drop of blood to appear on his cheek where the bar of his helm left him unprotected.

"Come then you Centaur filth, you think you can defeat me? You are not even half a man, more beast than man!" Keron shouted, flecks of spittle flying from his mouth as he watched Beru turn and prepare to charge him.

"Better a beast than the father of a weakling!" Beru said smiling as he moved slower this time towards Keron, his eyes locked onto that of the human king's, enrapturing him with their beauty, spellbinding him with the magic of the fey that Centaurs possessed

"Your time has come, Keron." He said as he raised his sword and slammed it down on the head of the King of Belline. With the force of the blow his helmet split, the blade biting deep into the bone of Keron's skull and his brain. Keron's neck snapped and he crumpled to the ground as Beru reared up on his hind legs and brought his forelegs crashing down on the body of Keron, his hooves clanging against the armour as it dented again and again as Beru struck the broken body of King Keron.

The Centaur king pulled his blade free with a sickening slurping sound as Keron's crushed skull relinquished the blade that killed him to its master. Beru's skin and hide was sweat-streaked and bloodied as he spat on the body in a final insult and turned to find another allied enemy to defeat.

***

Aderon and the others searched the bustling and bloodied battlefield striking against Imps and Orcs, felling them with their desperate blows in the search for Keron. The sharp eyes of the Dwarven king saw the battered crest of the King's breastplate.

"There!" he said and surged forward, striking a Centaur's hind legs from beneath it as it reared to strike at another human soldier, the Centaur fell to the ground and was set upon by a nearby soldier to claim the kill. The enemy soldiers retreated to their lines while the battered allied southern army regrouped and pushed them forward to keep their remaining kings safe.

11

"He has passed." The Dwarven king said as he drew his dagger, there was no blood or broken skin on the dead king as his crumpled body lay in the churned earth of the battlefield. Halven pierced the hand of Keron and pressed a drop of blood from his cooling fingers.

The Magician took the crystal to the drop of blood and it changed colour to a deep crimson and warmed in his hands as his companion wizard fell to the ground, the life energies going to the crystal to activate the spell, all that remained was to cast it.

"It is ready." The magician said as he turned to the Kings.

"Then it is time." Aderon said.

"And not a moment too soon." Var said as he looked towards the regrouping enemy.

Beru called out across the bloodied and churned mud of the battlefield to the Kings and Magicians.

"Pray to whatever gods will listen, Kings of the South, for your bodies will join those whom I have myself trampled beneath my hooves. Your broken bodies will feed the maggots and carrion eaters of this world while your souls will find their eternal torment at the hands of the denizens of the underworld!" his voice carried across the battlefield, over the moans of the mortally wounded, the bodies of the dead, and those injured who were trying to crawl back to their lines in desperation for healing and survival.

The Centaur King laughed as he raised his bloodied sword high, eliciting a great war-cry from his armies that broke across the field in a thundering wave of sound.

"Magician, when he charges, cast the spell." Adeon said, a hand placed upon the shoulder of his magician.

"Yes, my king." The magician said nodding, as he held the crystal in both hands, shaking with the fear that ran through his body.

A war cry broke free from Beru's lips as he led the charge. His men and their allies surged forward after him in a mass of bloodthirsty bodies, bent on slaughter and victory. Bloodied mud flew up under hooves and booted feet as they came in for what would be the final breaking charge.

"Cast it, cast it now!" Aderon shouted at the magician, as he pulled his sword from its scabbard, ready to defend himself should their spell fail. He felt the surge of magic run through his veins as the magician cast one of the most powerful spells ever created. Each king felt the building power of the crystal as the magic unfurled. The crystal began to glow a brilliant red as the Magician continued to chant the spell.

Aderon watched in awe as Beru bore down on him, the Centaur skidded to a stop before him, the earth ramming over his blood stained hooves. He reared up over Aderon, his sword drawn back and his face a mask of deadly glee as he prepared to strike.

With a speed that belied his age, the old magician stepped in front of Beru, and thrust the luminescent red

13

crystal into the equine chest of the Centaur. A blank, leather bound book in his hands as he began to incant the final casting of the powerful spell. Brilliant words glowed upon the page, as he spoke the words to cast the final part of the spell the words burned magically into the parchment pages of the book.

"I cast you and your fey army and peoples out of this Realm, Beru of the Centaurs! Be gone from this place!" the magician chanted in an arcane language, fumbling one or two words as his voice shook and his concentration faltered slightly with the fear that pulsed through is heart.

Beru was frozen in place, a fearsome, rearing pose as the gemstone lodged in his equine chest changed colour from deep red to purple, blue and then to black as the magic worked against the Centaur king and his soldiers.

Beru's body hardened, and inch by inch turned to a dark grey stone that resembled marble. This spell continued on through his front line soldiers. Each beast had turned into a stone statue beside their Centaur King. As the crystal in his chest changed colour, it hummed in increasing volume and wisps of purple, blue and red lights entwined themselves around Beru's body, forming a funnel of light, not unlike that of a tornado.

"Back my lords, lets we get caught in the banishing spell!" the magician warned, taking a brief pause from his arcane chanting as he stepped back. King Var turned to his men and shouted the retreat.

In a flurry of armoured bodies, the armies of the South retreated while the noise of the crystal grew ever louder and the swirling lights brighter.

"We should be safe here my lords!" the magician shouted over the noise of the crystal's hum before he continued his chanting. They stopped and turned to watch as a huge vortex formed above the battlefield.

One by one each enemy soldier who still lived or hadn't turned to stone was taken up in a flash of light into the vortex, soon the flashes joined to form one huge beam of light, that grew so bright that it pained those who gazed upon it.

As the magician finished his arcane chanting, a thunderclap erupted across the skies, its rumble echoing across the lands. When those who had cowered from the thunderous peal looked to the skies, they saw the vortex had vanished, to be replaced by an aurora of reds, purples and blues across a black sky.

"My Lords." The magician said, his voice filled with the utter and complete exhaustion that showed in his face. "They have been banished to another realm, all the Centaurs and their allies, every last one. The spell that was cast is in this book, as is the breaking spell" He took a breath and steadied himself as he held the book out to Aderon. "But there is a problem, I had a vision as I cast the spell." He looked worried as the King of the elves took the spell book from his shaking hands.

"What is it wise one?" Aderon asked with reverence for the Magician's sacrifice.

"They will return, in two thousand years the Centaurs and their allies will return to this world… they will be released by an idiot, and there will be bloody war."

Chapter One.

Chilly water struck him with a force that caused Griffon to suck in his breath, and a good mouthful of water followed it into his lungs. He coughed and spluttered as he sat up in the filth of the cobblestone-lined gutter in Stone Street in Hestone.

"You're a useless piece of garbage Griffon du Frain!" Pearl screeched at him from her door, the leather bucket in hand. "Get off my doorstep or I'll call the constabulary. Why I took you in only the Gods know. Fool I was." She slammed the door shut, the noise hammering against the hangover headache he was sporting.

A minutes passed as he blinked against the glaringly bright morning sun. A sack of his meagre possessions dropped to the cobbled path beside the gutter from Pearl's first floor window where her bedroom was. It was now obvious that in his still-drunken state last night he had come home only to find comfort not in Pearl's arms, or her bed, but the muddy and foul smelling gutter instead.

Now Pearl had thrown him out, and he knew it was coming but he had hoped that he could be indulged just a little bit longer. He lifted his head and noticed that the reek that surrounded him was not only of the gutter, he smelled of whore and cheap alcohol. Pearl was a whore herself, but she was a jealous whore, and could not abide any women touching whichever man she considered to be hers. Of all her choices, Griffon du Frain was one of the worst.

He had no job, and a bad gambling and drinking problem. They had argued many times over him spending what little money he earned, when he had work, on alcohol and games of chance. He much preferred to sleep away the days in her bed, while reserving the nights for gambling and drinking, often carousing with his friends until the early hours of the morning. Most nights he would make it home, or he would find himself sleeping it off in the cells at the Constabulary office.

Griffon wrinkled his nose and felt his stomach roil in response. He heaved twice before he purged his stomach of the soured drink from the night before, adding to the mess in the gutter that already covered him. Retching again, Griffon hawked and spat the last sour dribbles of bile from his mouth before he staggered to his feet.

Griffon was lucky that he had not been picked up by the constabulary, though it would have made for a far more comfortable night sleeping in the dry cells, but he could not afford the fine or the bail. He collected his sack and made a rude gesture up at Pearl's whore's den before he staggered away from the little hovel he had called home for the last two months.

Griffon wandered the streets not caring where he went, until he heard a curt whistle behind him.

"'ello Griff ol' son." Mouse said as Griffon turned to see who whistled him.

"Oh… Mouse, I was just on my way to come and see Jimmy…" Griffon said, smiling uneasily.

"Really?" Mouse said as he rocked back on his heels and then forward to the balls of his feet, hands clasped before him, and thumbs twiddling together, "Well, that's a stroke o' luck then ain't it, 'cause word on the street is you got tossed outta that whore's house this fine mornin'" Mouse said as he grinned around the small sliver of wood he was always seen to be chewing.

"I see word travels fast on the street." Griffon mused.

"Indeed, it does. I got my little sources here there 'n' everywhere!" Mouse said with a wicked grin. "It pays to know things." He smirked.

"Look, I've got your money… err… that is to say…" Griffon started.

"You'll get my money…?" Mouse said with a raised eyebrow, finishing Griffon's half-arsed excuse for him.

Griffon nodded. Mouse grinned with a wicked gleam in his eye and shook his head.

"Not this time, sunshine. Boss is awful tired of you dodgin' your payments, so now you gotta deal with me an' my lads." Mouse said as he put two fingers to his mouth and whistled. Two big bully boys came around the corner and grinned as they stood a step behind Mouse. Their demeanour unmistakably threatening.

"Get 'im, lads." Mouse said, chewing around the slip of wood in his mouth.

Griffon turned and ran down the street, ducking around the early morning shoppers, the tow bully boys in hot pursuit. "Can't run forever boy!" one shouted out to him.

"Stop an' take it like a man!" shouted the other as they charged past a little old lady with a basket filled with bread, knocking her aside as they ran past. The old shrew went down with a startled cry and a foul curse at the two bully boys as her bread fell onto the dirty street

Griffon rounded a corner, he knew this town like the back of his hand, but he wasn't thinking and turned into an alleyway that ran behind the butchers, it was also a dead end.

"Got ya now, boy-o." said a gravelly voice behind him.

Griffon turned into the first punch aimed at the back of his head. Soon he felt the agony of more blows landing on his body, and then, mercifully, nothing as his vision faded to black.

#

Griffon's body was a mass of aches and pains and a glorious number of bruises.

He woke up, barely able to open one eye, as the other had swollen shut, the lid was crusted over with dried blood and mucus. His lips were split and swollen, and his mouth felt like it was filled with lamb's wool. He was certain they had knocked a tooth loose. He groaned when he sat up, his head spinning and then groaned even louder when he found himself in the constable's cells.

"Mornin' there Griffon." Constable Odal mumbled from around his pipe. The acrid blue smoke hovered in a haze above the balding constable's head.

"Bugger off… can't you see I'm in a world of pain here?" Griffon mumbled and flopped himself back down onto the rough straw mattress, rolling over so his back was to the Dwarven constable.

"Ooh that's nice language for a man come into a nice bit of inheritance, I'd have thought with the change in your circumstance you might allow yourself a might bit more decorum, considering the land and wealth you now have." The constable said with a chuckle.

Griffon rolled back over to look at him.

"What are you talking about?" he said with curiosity in his voice.

The constable held up a roll of parchment with a black seal on it.

"Your Grandfather is dead." He tossed the roll into Griffon's cell, not even bothering to get up. He tapped out the ashes from his pipe and repacked fresh tobacco in to the bowl before he lit a taper from the lone candle on the desk and continued to puff away.

Griffon groaned as he got to his feet and moaned as he leaned down to grab the scroll from the cold stone floor, his vision swam and the cell spun around him. Griffon kept his footing and his state of consciousness. He broke the black seal and through blurry vision was just able to make out the elegant longhand of Nirimanye, his Grandfather's Elven housemaid.

"Griffon, it is my dearest hope that this letter finds you well and safe. I write to you to inform you that your Grandfather passed away in his home after a long illness.

He has bequeathed his home, lands and possessions to you, to keep for you and your progeny for as long as the family line holds.

Please, I know that you and he were oft quarrelling with each other, and I know not what caused your estrangement with him, but he loved you and you were his only family, I truly wish that you had set aside your differences and been a family again before he passed. His last thoughts were of you, and he felt great regret that you and he were still estranged.

You know where the house is, I will be there taking care of things for you for your return home.

Please, come home.

Nirimanye.

Griffon couldn't believe his luck, he knew his Grandfather had plenty of old, but valuable junk that he could sell. His financial troubles were surely behind him now! He could pay off his money lender, and go out drinking and carousing with his friends to celebrate.

"Hey! Constable, let me out would you?" he said as he clutched the scroll in a hand with bloodied, swollen and bruised fingers, he grabbed the bars, the scroll crumpling slightly in his hand.

The dwarf looked at him over the end of his pipe.

"Now why would I do that? Just so you can go out and start fighting again?" he grinned and shook his head. "Nah I don't think so, you're less trouble in the cell than out of it Griffon. Tomorrow we might let you out, but you'll have the fine to pay." The Dwarf said as he picked up a sheath of parchment and wrote on it, dipping the fine pigeon feather quill into the inkwell. The *scratch-scratch-scratch* of the quill on parchment grated against the remnants of Griffon's hangover and his beating induced headache. Despite several pleas for his release, the constable and his subsequent relief refused to let him go and Griffon had to resign himself to another night in the cells.

***

Dawn broke through the barred window and warmed his face. The clanking of keys against the bars of the cell as the constable unlocked the door roused him from his slumber. Griffon got up stiff and sore, his body protesting the movement. He opened his swollen eye and blinked it a few times to clear the slight blur in his vision.

"All right Griffon, time to leave us, someone paid up your bond." The constable said as he opened the door of the cell. Griffon walked out with a wide grin, keeping it on his face until he walked out into the street and saw who had paid his bond,

23

"'ello Sunshine, have a nice stay at 'is majesty's finest?" Mouse said with a grin as he leaned against a stone wall. "You owe us double now, you got 'till sundown to get it. Got it?" Griffon nodded.

"You'll have it by sundown." He said, nodding his head in agreement.

"Good, 'cause if ya don't, I'll have ya swinging from the hangin' tree soon after sundown." Mouse said as he sauntered away.

Griffon went in the opposite direction, taking the road that led out of Hestone and towards his Grandfather's farm.

The sun felt good on his back, easing the muscles that were bruised from his beating. He whistled a nameless tune as he walked along, joining other travellers on the road from Hestone to the sea port of Swaford.

As he walked he noticed a figure in the distance. The heat shimmer from the road ahead hid the figure as it approached him on horseback. Griffon and some of the other travellers shifted to the side of the road as the figure drew closer.

The cloaked and hooded man rode past Griffon and the other travellers without so much as a 'Good morning' thrown their way, Griffon watched after him, his figure receding into the distance towards Hestow before he turned back to his own journey.

It took a good hour on foot to get to the farm, and he decided that on his return to the town, he would buy a horse

to make travelling a bit easier. Perhaps he would even hire…
no *buy* a carriage and hire a driver. That would show that
silly whore, Pearl who was useless!

Griffon grinned as he thought of arriving at Pearl's
den in a luxurious carriage and dressed like a nobleman,
preening like a peacock, and showing off a lovely young
courtesan on his arm, he stopped and wondered where he
might find a courtesan at such short notice.

He forgot the notion as soon as he saw the
farmhouse, memories of his childhood returning.

It was a little thatch roofed cottage, two stories with
tiny glass windows that poked through the thatch roof where
the attic was.

White smoke drifted up through a river-stone
chimney, and stones from the same riverbed formed the
outer walls of the cottage. There was a vegetable patch to
one side and as he walked he could hear the clucking of
chickens. A few black and white cows grazed in a nearby
paddock, one with a calf at her feet, and a nanny goat with a
full udder was tethered to a tree near the woodshed, her
interest was on the yellow daisies scattered about the ground
and how quickly she could devour them and not the new lord
of the farm.

He came up to the house and pushed on the door, it
opened without protest.

"Hello?" he called as he entered, his boots leaving
muddy prints as he walked over an old rug that covered the
worn floorboards. He smelled something warm and hearty

cooking in a pot over the low coals of the fire. His mouth watered, and he spied something covered in a cloth napkin sitting on the table.

Griffon pulled the napkin from the platter, a wedge of cheese, fresh bread and two thick slices of cold ham, along with some pickled onions and cucumbers arranged ever-so-delightfully on the plate. His mouth watered with the savoury scents of the ham and the tangy vinegar used to pickle the onions and cucumbers.

He sat down and tore a hunk of bread from the small loaf on the plate and set to, having not eaten anything for a good day and a half and only remembering how hungry he was when he had smelled the food.

The platter was empty before he knew it and he belched, pleased with such a meal and grateful that someone had the forethought to put it out for him, which made him wonder if Nirimanye had known he was coming. He wiped his mouth on the napkin and tossed it onto the empty platter.

Griffon went upstairs to his Grandfather's room, his boots tracking more mud through the little house. There were three rooms, one was empty but for a simple bed and dresser, with a chair beside it and had been his when he was a young lad.

He had left the house at fifteen after an argument with his Grandfather over something that he himself couldn't even remember. Now seven years later he was back in the old man's house and it still smelled the same, just like his Grandfather, old beeswax, but with another underlying, but ageless scent that he could never identify.

Griffon pulled an old wooden chair under the trapdoor that led to the attic of the old house and yanked on the rope, releasing the trapdoor. As it opened, the ladder rolled out on its mechanism and smacked him soundly on the head, Griffon swore as he lost his balance and fell off the chair, landing hard on his ass. He grumbled as he picked himself up and rubbed at the angry lump that was now forming on his head.

The dark opening of the attic yawned wide at him, calling him to come and explore the treasures that his Grandfather had hidden from him. With a determined grunt, Griffon reset the chair and climbed up the ladder and into the gloom of the attic.

Dust cloths covered boxes and chests in the attic and Griffon set to pulling them off and uncovering the fabulous treasures that were hidden inside. The gleam of a set of daggers, with golden hilts inlaid with precious jewels caught his eye, complete with scabbards. He grinned as he pulled them out and put them in a sack. Silver goblets and gold platters followed, there would be plenty of stuff here to sell and pay back Mouse with, and with some left over to go out and celebrate his good fortune with the boys.

With a sack filled with trinkets and treasures, he clambered down the ladder and left the house, heading down the road and to town, his pace joyously quick and the delight shining on his face, despite the bruised muscles and the sack heavy with items to sell.

Chapter Two.

Nirimanye breathed in the fresh air as she walked behind the horse-drawn plough. The blade furrowed the soil, but the soil was hard with the dry season that they had endured, but the work kept her busy and her mind peaceful. She had wept the loss of Ter, he had been like a father to her, Ter was not just her guardian, but a friend and mentor. She had known him for most of his life.

Now he was gone and a grandson whom she'd not seen in seven years, was the owner of this land and the inheritor of a great but honourable burden. She wondered what he was like and if life had been as kind to him as it had to her.

She decided that it was definitely time for a break, noon had come and gone and she had missed it in the determination to get as much of the work done as she possibly could. She brushed her sweaty hands over her dress and took the horse from the traces of the plough, leading the large animal back to the farmhouse, hitching the mare to the post by the barn door and letting her drink from the large water trough beside the barn before she went to the well and drew a bucket of clean water to wash her hands and face in.

Feeling much cleaner and better for her efforts, Nirimanye walked to the house and pushed open the door. Muddy boot prints greeted her, she followed the boot prints to the table where her lunch platter was empty of her hard-earned and lovingly prepared lunch. She looked around the kitchen and jumped when she heard a noise upstairs. She turned and ran out of the farmhouse and made for the barn.

She grabbed the wickedly sharp hand-scythe that she and Ter had used when it was time to cut the wheat crop. Now armed with the sharp steel and with a little bravery running through her veins, she braved the intruder in the house.

She crept quietly up the stairs, pausing when she hit the eighth step, as she knew it would creak, she slowly let her weight down on the old, creaky stair before she let the held breath that she held in anxiety free, the stair stayed silent much to her relief. She continued on towards the bedrooms and peeked in each open door before she found to her shock that Ter's room was where the noises had come from, evidenced by the open trapdoor that led to the attic. It sometimes fell open when the house warmed in the sunshine and the wood warped, but she could never be too careful, for there were a few brigands about.

With a bravery that she didn't particularly feel, Nirimanye slowly climbed up the ladder and into the gloom. There was no-one there. She sighed and retreated back down the ladder. With some effort she managed to push the trap door back in its proper position. She smoothed down the simple dress she wore for her work and headed back downstairs. She served herself a far simpler meal than what she had originally prepared for herself, the meal that had been mysteriously eaten, and headed back out to finish the day's work before she lost too many hours to this mystery.

***

Griffon laughed heartily with his mates in the pub. Empty tankards and mugs surrounded them and barmaids scurried to refill the pewter mugs. Women of the Tavern were drawn to the glitter of Griffon's coin and swooned

29

around him. As soon as Tom and Jack heard he had coin, they stuck to him like flies to horse biscuits. Griffon bought each round, and of course, Tom and Sam weren't in a position to refuse him. Soon deep in their merry cups, Griffon forgot the main reason why he had the money, until he saw Mouse.

"'ello Sunshine," he said with a smile. "Got my money?" Mouse reached forward and grabbed Griffon by the collar of his fancy new clothes he had bought from the tailors, his mug of ale spilled down his fine trousers leaving a mark that looked like he had pissed himself.

"Been spending it have ya?" Mouse said to Griffon, his foul breath turning Griffon's stomach with the proximity of the moneylender to the young man's face. Mouse shook Griffon hard, hearing the few coins he had left jingling in the leather purse at his side made the moneylender's bruiser smile.

"Music to my ears," Mouse said as he cut the purse from Griffon's belt, and put it inside his tunic for safekeeping. "But this, this is not good enough, I want triple now, you got until sunset boy, get to it!" Mouse said with a smirk. "Mind you hurry home now Griffon, else I'll have to send my lads around to your new lodgings, and they will take five times what you owe." Griffon gulped and nodded before Mouse threw him to the ground. Griffon watched from the filthy pub floor as Mouse shoved Tom and Sam aside and drank his ale, pulling the drink hard down his throat and ignoring the overflow as it trickled down to soak his filthy collar. Mouse turned from the bar and glared down at Griffon,

"Move it scum…" he said gruffly, as he kicked a scuffed leather boot into Griffon's bruised ribs. Griffon coughed painfully into his hand, blood from his re-split lip smeared across his fingers. He quickly crawled away from the reach of Mouse's boot before he got to his feet and ran with a hobbling gait for the farmhouse, knocking the beer from a patron's hand, he stammered out and apology as he bolted.

The bearded man looked at his now empty hand as the mug clattered on the ground watched the hapless fellow as he stumbled out the door and fell on his face into the dirty street. Griffon cursed and got back to his feet and ran down the street back towards his Grandfather's house

Griffon had never run so far or so fast in his life. He was exhausted, panting and bathed in sweat by the time he got to the farmhouse. But the threat of Mouse having him strung up and hanging until his throat closed with the tightness of the noose finally hit him. He burst through the door of the farmhouse and ran up the stairs in a panicked clatter of muddy boots. He leapt for the rope on the trapdoor and pulled it down, the ladder sliding home to hit the floor with a loud thud as it hit the floor.

Griffon was up the ladder and in the attic faster than he could blink. He scrounged through the items in his Grandfather's attic, finding only dull swords and dented armour, he sobbed when he realised that he had been overly greedy and had only taken the beautiful shiny and pretty items, selling them for whatever he could get. There were a few books in a box but nothing that he would consider worth selling, until his eyes cast upon one ornately carved box.

'Surely there must be something quite valuable in here!' he thought to himself as he flipped open the brass catches. Inside was a beautifully preserved, but quite plain leatherbound book. The case was lined with red velvet, the book lay on the bottom of the box on its' own velvet pillow.

Griffon's curiosity got the better of him and he opened the old book, forgetting about his bloodied fingers. The smell of age, and dust greeted him as he opened the cover to look at the front pages of the tome. His dark eyes roamed over the ancient language. As he tried to read, he noticed that he could smell something else in the air too, something powerful and ancient, it tasted of power and danger. His eyes took in the now-glowing words on the page and he understood the words. Surge of power flowed through his body from his bloodied fingers from the book. With his understanding of the language, something compelled him to read it aloud. Part of his mind fought for control as he felt panic rising in him, something wasn't right.

His mouth opened, lips parted, tongue moving as he began to speak strange archaic words, words that felt and tasted of a great and terrible power, one that had waited millennia to break free from a prison, one that stank of anger and revenge, of beings ancient and determined in their quest, but what that quest was, he didn't know. He cried out the last word as a wave of power burst out from the book, rattling the windows and shaking the thatch in the roof.

Griffon fell to the floor, unconscious.

***

Nirimanye strained with the heavy axe above her head, a small pile of chopped wood already lay at her feet as she continued her work around the farm. The strange occurrences in the little farmhouse played on her mind, she knew someone had been in the house, but her check of the attic had revealed nothing, the boxes had appeared undisturbed but she had hardly ventured up there, even when Ter was alive. What was up there was Ter's business.

She let the axe drop heavily onto the upright log, splitting it slightly and jamming the axe head in the wood. She was about to raise the wood laden axe again to finish the split when she heard a voice drifting on the breeze. Nirimanye turned to face the sound, the little farm house stood stoically and quiet as it usually had, apart from the voice drifting on the wind from the open window of the attic.

Nirimanye walked towards the house, dropping the axe to the ground as she headed towards the door. She could feel the power in the words that she heard whispered on the wind. She could sense the electrifying magic that it invoked and she felt a small knot of fear in her heart, an instinctual fear of something that she could not name, but knew that it didn't bode well. She picked up her pace and began to run towards the house only to be knocked backwards to the ground when a huge pulse of energy washed over her.

She got up slowly and shook her head to clear the panoply of stars that cascaded over her vision. When she felt steady enough to continue she moved quickly back towards the cottage and through the door.

The acrid tang of ancient and powerful magic assailed her nose as she climbed the stairs, grabbing a sharp kitchen knife as she passed the preparation table. There were things that she knew of in the attic that were of a magical nature and Ter had kept them up there as he was one of the very few in this world who knew of their true natures. She swallowed her fear and climbed the ladder of the once again open trapdoor to the attic.

The gloom greeted her, only the small open window offering any sort of light in the attic. She held the little knife out before her as she came around a large chest, some things were missing and she inwardly cursed, she should have come up to check the last time she thought she had heard a noise.

She scanned the area as her eyes adjusted to the light, finally settling on a body that lay before a chest with a book that was nestled inside. Her eyes scanned over the pages but she could not read it. She looked from the pages of the strange book to the body that lay on the floor. She nudged the soft arm of the man with the toe of her leather boot, he groaned and moved, opening his eyes slightly before he closed them again.

Nirimanye crouched down and looked at him, he had a similar face to Ter, apart from the black and blue bruising and the swelling surely this beaten sack of potatoes could not be Ter's heir? She shook her head and kicked him again.

"Get up, Thief or I'll send for the constabulary." She said with a voice that shook slightly.

"Mmm…not…thief…" the man grumbled as he tried to open his eyes.

"What did you say?" Nirimanye said, prodding him again in a particularly tender spot on his side. The man yelped and grabbed his side.

"Get up." Nirimanye repeated. "Thieves are not welcome here."

"I'm not a thief." The fellow said with a protesting, whining tone as he slowly got to his knees and ran a hand over his aching face, he opened his eyes and looked at her.

"Then what are you doing here in this house?" Nirimanye asked him holding the knife out with an unsteady hand, in what she hoped was a sufficiently threatening gesture.

"This is my house." The man said as he slowly sat up, wincing as he felt the pull of bruised muscles. "My Grandfather left it to me."

"Griffon…?" Nirimanye asked in wonder. "You've changed… quite a bit." She said observing his efforts to get to his feet, she set down her knife and helped him to stand.

"Well we aren't all long lived peoples like Elves or Dwarves, you haven't changed a bit since I left." He said with a weary smile as he swayed on his feet a little.

"What happened up here?" she asked looking around at the little signs of chaos that surrounded them.

"I uh… needed some things." He said rubbing the back of his neck awkwardly.

"Needed some things? Like what?" she asked looking into his eyes and seeing the guilty glint to them.

"Just… some things…" he said mumbling a little.

"Griffon," Nirimanye said as she took him by the shoulders and looked at his battered face. "Are you in trouble?"

"I… owe some people some money," he said sheepishly, Nirimanye rolled her eyes in disgust. "Look, my life hasn't been the best. In the last two days my woman threw me out on the street, I've been attacked, beaten up and locked in the constabulary's cells. I just learned yesterday that my Grandfather died and left me the farm." Griffon said as he sat down on a crate.

"Well…" Nirimanye didn't know what else to say, she put her hands on her hips and sighed, thinking on what to do with him. "Come downstairs, I'll clean you up and get you fed." She said softly, knowing that she owed Ter and his family a lot, she also held many of the family's secrets close to her heart, as she herself was one of them.

She helped him down the ladder and the stairs and put a small pot of water on to boil before she went and gathered some herbs from the garden to brew a soothing tea and also a bathing solution to clear the blood and scabs from his beatings, then she bound his bruised ribs with fresh linen bandages.

She served a plate of stew for him and then went about gathering him some clothes from his Grandfather's wardrobe. She ate quickly while he changed.

"Well." Griffon said as he sat down after he had cleaned and changed into clothes that smelled of a mixture of lavender soap and old man. "I guess this is home…" he said as he looked at a mug of cider that Nirimanye set before him.

Chapter Three

Sir Hugh moved along the road, visiting Hestone had given him the confirmation that their Grand Master Knight had passed on, and that his grandson was the heir to the power that could keep the threat at bay. They had been preparing for the last two thousand years for this, and Hugh just hoped that Ter had prepared the young man.

Sir Hugh had been out of the Kingdom of Vallonde for twenty years, travelling along the roads and serving the people of the Iron Kingdom, and Beline in issues of justice where the local constabularies would refuse to mediate, or just the smaller villages that were difficult to get to. He mediated issues of clan wars amongst the dwarves, matters of service and indenture, disputes of honour, it was what the Knights of Erandia were there for, along with the protection of a great and terrible spell.

He felt something in the air, it pushed hard against him, a wave of power, a force of magic that made him stagger in his step. Every hair on the back of his neck stood up with the sense of wrongness that came with the magical wave that washed over him.

He looked to the north where on a clear day you could just see the aurora in the darkened sky above the March of the Damned where the stone statues of the Centaur war host still stood today. The day was certainly clear enough, but there were clouds to the far north above the Darklands, so it was pointless to try to see the colours that heralded the magical energies that held a dangerous enemy entrapped behind them.

He pulled his cloak around him tighter, feeling a sudden chill to the air as he continued on to the farm that once belonged to Ter at a leisurely pace.

He arrived an hour before dusk and pushed his way through the old gate, past the clucking chickens and the grazing nanny goat, to the thatched roof cottage where warm lights shone through the windows and a smell of something savoury teased his nose, making his mouth water and his stomach rumble in anticipation of a good meal and hopefully fine company.

He reached the door and knocked on the old wood panels. He heard muffled voices inside, a woman's, and a man's, the man sounded panicked as he heard footsteps approaching the door. With a click the latch was released and the door opened, Sir Hugh smiled and bowed his head to the Elf who opened the door.

"My Lady," he said with his head lowered, "I am Sir Hugh of the Knights of Erandia, I have come to pay my respects to the old Grand Master Knight, and have come to renew my vows to the new Grand Master..." Sir Hugh trailed off as he looked beyond the doorframe and saw a young man cowering behind a chair.

"Please, come in Sir Knight, you are welcome in the home of the Grand Master." The Elven woman said, as she stepped aside to let Sir Hugh in. The knight looked around the simple home and sat in a chair offered by the Elven lady, a platter of hot stew and bread was placed before him and he thanked her for the hospitality before he began to eat. The young man came out from behind the seat and settled nervously in the chair.

"Are you all right there, lad?" Sir Hugh asked the fellow as he shook in the seat.

"Yes... fine, just fine." The man said with a voice that showed that he was not 'fine, just fine'. Sir Hugh watched him steadily, his nervous disposition was grating on his own nerves and he wondered what the lad had done to make himself so tightly wound.

Nirimanye came up and placed a mug of cider before Sir Hugh and smiled, "Griffon is a bit worried about some local bullies coming to bash his head in," she said, explaining the lad's nerves.

"Oh, got in a spot of bother there, lad?" Hugh asked with a laugh. "Never mind, I'm sure you can handle them, you are after all a Knight... aren't you?" The look that Griffon gave him back made him almost choke on the stew. He looked good and hard at the lad before he realised that he was the one who had knocked against him and made him drop his beer in the tavern.

"A Knight?" Griffon replied, and shook his head. "No, not a knight, just a fool, plain and simple." Griffon said sadly.

"What your Grandfather never taught you the ways of the Knighthood of Erandia? Never made you his squire?" Sir Hugh asked with surprise in his voice, though it explained the young man's demeanour towards strangers knocking at the door. A Knight would not be nearly pissing his pants in fear of the knocking at the door by a stranger, nor would a Knight have gotten himself in such a terrible position that this idiot had.

"Right. From the start, boy, tell me everything…" Sir Hugh said as he turned in his chair to face the young man, his voice showing that he meant for Griffon to tell him *everything*.

Griffon gulped the last of his cider and began his woeful tale, from the start, his estrangement from his Grandfather when he became a man, leaving home right through to his gambling and drinking problems, getting thrown out of the house he shared with Pearl the whore, right up to going through the attic for things to sell.

Hugh sighed and pinched the bridge of his nose with forefinger and thumb as he wondered how many priceless treasures the boy had unwittingly pilfered, then he came across a very troubling thought.

"Tell me, was there a book amongst the things you sold?" Hugh asked, "A really old book?" he leaned forward and looked at the young man.

"No… I don't think so… no wait, there was, but I didn't take it, I swear!" Griffon said, his eyes wide and innocent.

"Did you… did you read it?" Sir Hugh asked, somehow already knowing the answer with a sick feeling in the pit of his stomach.

"No... Maybe... I'm not sure..." Griffon said in confusion, "I just remember waking up on the floor with Nirimanye kicking me."

"I never kicked you, I poked you with the toe of my boot and maybe threatened you with a knife a little, but what was I supposed to think with a strange man in the house!" Nirimanye said as she washed up the dishes in a bucket of water with scrubbing sand.

Sir Hugh was on his feet in a second.

"Show me the book." He said, his voice shaking.

"What... Now?" Griffon asked, Nirimanye had just set a peach pie down on the table with fresh cream for their dessert.

Sir Hugh leaned down on the table, knuckles curled under hands and placed on the wooden tabletop, his eyes hard on Griffon's, making him feel uncomfortable.

"Right. Fogging. Now." He said each word with more than a hint of venom.

Griffon was on his feet and up the stairs before Sir Hugh had moved to follow him

The gloom of the attic had changed to a point where a candle was required to see and not stumble over anything that had been shifted in Griffon's first rummage for loot to sell.

Sir Hugh followed him to where the book lay open.

"The vision that the wizard had has come true... *The spell will be broken... by an idiot'*." Sir Hugh said softly.

"Hey!" Griffon said indignantly. "I'm not an idiot... wait... what spell?" he asked curious.

"The Spell that bound the entire army of the Darklands, Centaurs, Minotaurs, Orcs, Goblins, all those creatures that no longer live in this realm. The ones that are now told as tales to get naughty children to behave. Two thousand years ago they existed, and wanted to take the world for themselves, enslaving the peoples of the south. The kingdoms of Men, Elves, and Dwarves were put under threat." Sir Hugh said as he ran his fingers over the arcane language of the book.

"The allied kingdoms of the south held them back, barely, with just enough time to cast a great and powerful spell that cost the lives of all but one of the southern realms' wizards. Thousands of soldiers of the allied armies died trying to keep them from achieving their goal. Now, because of you, they will return, regroup and come to make war again. But this time, they will not stop until they have what they want, and their revenge will be bloody." He finished.

"Your Grandfather should have told you all this when you took up a place as his squire." Sir Hugh said stiffly.

"I didn't see eye to eye with my Grandfather on a lot of things so I left when I turned fifteen, as I told you." Griffon said. Sir Hugh looked grim.

"The next year on your sixteenth birthday would have been when he took you as his squire." Sir Hugh said softly. He leaned forward and closed up the book, wrapping it back up in its velvet covers and closing the lid of its box, snapping the latch shut.

"Well, there is nothing for it, we have been preparing for this for a long time, I must call my brother knights, and we must discuss what to do." He turned to Griffon. "I hate to say it lad, but you are one of the few people on this world who can save us from the Centaur Armies."

Griffon looked sick. "Me?"

"Yes, you. It has been foretold in the prophecy, you will break the spell, and release the Centaur King's army, but you will also end the coming war. Though how, I do not know" Sir Hugh said as he picked up the box containing the book and headed down the ladder.

Nirimanye was busy sweeping the floors when Hugh and Griffon came downstairs.

"My Lady, I need your help, I will be calling a moot of the Knights in order to try to finalise the preparations that we have been making for the last two thousand years, May I use one of the empty fields to host them?" he asked her.

"Of course, Sir Hugh. How many knights are we expecting?" Nirimanye asked as she swept up the dust and threw it into the fire.

"About fifty, plus a number of squires." Sir Hugh explained. Nirimanye thought for a moment.

44

"Come with me." She said as she put away the broom and headed to a small door that led to the cellar.

"Ter showed me this years ago, he told me that if ever there was a moot, that the Knights would be housed in here." She said as she walked down the stairs, taking a lantern and lighting it with a taper that she had lit from one of the candles that stood flickering by the door. Warm golden light illuminated the cellar, it was small with a few shelves lining the walls filled with preservatives and supplies for the house.

"How are you going to fit fifty knights in here?" Griffon asked, following down the stone steps.

"Not in here, silly," Nirimanye said with a grin as she moved one of the empty shelves aside, Sir Hugh moved to help her shift the wooden shelf away, revealing the old door hidden behind it.

"In here…" she said as she stepped back she pushed hard on the door, the old hinges protesting the movement from their stillness. She grabbed a candle and taper, and stepped over the threshold. As she passed them, Nirimanye lit the lanterns that hung along one side of the wall. The room opened out to reveal a line of sheet covered racks.

Sir Hugh moved to one and pulled the heavily-oiled sheet off, it dropped to the ground, revealing a neatly stacked and stored line of swords, in pristine condition, sharp and serviceable. He murmured in approval, as he moved to the next lot of racks, unstrung bows with wax paper packages holding their strings were stacked and ready to be strung and used. Wooden boxes filled with finely fletched arrows lay

45

beside the racks along with empty quivers waiting to be filled with arrows.

Nirimanye moved on as Griffon followed her, lighting more lanterns as she went. The growing light revealing a workshop complete with forge, kitchen with mess hall and a barracks lined with single beds. The entire place was deeper underground than Griffon realised.

Sir Hugh followed them into the mess hall, lined with sturdy wooden tables.

"What is this place?" he asked in amazement.

"This was once a small fortress, but fire took out much of the old upper levels, and the stones that remained after the fire were cleared from the ruins. they were used to build Ter's cottage, and the barn and stables, some of the old fences as well." She explained.

"Ter said he was more than pleased to find that he had purchased such a fine bit of land, and that he had chosen to dig his cellar here, he didn't know the rest of the fort was here, but when he found the top of the old door, we spent many months digging it out, while we lived in an oilskin tent. Back then the cottage was just a drawing on parchment. You can guess our amazement at finding the lower levels still intact." She said smiling in the light of the lantern that flickered on the table.

"Yes, it's incredible." Sir Hugh agreed. He turned his gaze to Griffon, looking over the lad with the eye of a Knight who knew something needed to be done about his terrible lack of training. He stepped in front of the young man. Who was sitting at one of the tables, looking around the large room. Sir Hugh went to bended knee. Griffon's eyes widened, surely this stranger wasn't proposing to him? The reality was much, much worse.

"Griffon, this night I will take you as my squire, you are going to be the next Grand Master Knight or at least going to be on the way to it by the time I am finished with you, we have much to do." Sir Hugh said as he stood up and started to head out of the door back up to the main cottage

"What? Wait!" Griffon said as he scrambled after Sir Hugh, his protestations falling on deaf ears. "Look, I don't think I want to be a Knight, I don't want to die, or be killed or maimed, or lose an eye, how horrible would that be?!" Griffon said his voice almost at a shrieking pitch as he followed Sir Hugh, "Look, why can't you be the grand master, or whatever it is? I mean you have plenty of experience! I can't do this!" Nirimanye followed along at a more sedate pace, extinguishing the lanterns ad closing the doors as she went and closed the cellar door behind her as Griffon continued to splutter excuses.

"You can and you will lad, it's in your bloodlines, your heritage, your inheritance..." Sir Hugh said as they came up into the kitchen.

"Which now belongs to me..." the voice of Mouse made Griffon's face drain of colour and his blood run cold in his veins. Mouse and four of his bully boys were in the Kitchen, Mouse sitting quite happily with his filthy boots on the table, Sir Hugh's half-finished mug of cider in his hand and a superior smirk on his face.

47

"Ah… young Griffon, you forgetting something, Sunshine? Something you might have needed to do before sunset today?" Mouse said with a smirk.

"Uh…" Griffon stammered.

"Thought so. Boys…"

"Don't you dare move a fogging muscle." Sir Hugh said warningly, his hand going to his sword and drawing the steel in one smooth motion.

"I agree," Nirimanye said as she came up as well, an arrow drawn on a bow and aimed at Mouse's throat.

"Now, now, my pretty little lady." Mouse said with his hands raised and a charming smile on his face. "Put away that bow before you hurt someone."

"I am asking you nicely to leave my home." Nirimanye said sternly. "I only ask nicely once, then I get a bit angry." She switched her aim at one of the bully boys as he moved slightly. "I can reload very quickly if I need to, and have an arrow in each of your throats before the first man hits the ground." Her threat was not an idle one, the archery skills of the Elves was legendary, and many of their scattered numbers found work as rangers on the hunting reserves of nobility. "There's a lovely lime pit out the back where I throw my rubbish, I am sure your bodies will go nicely towards helping to fertilise the fields come planting season."

"Okay my dear, put the bow down. We just want the runt there." Mouse said pointing an upraised hand, "He owes

48

me a lot of money, you see, not good to have debits to people, I'm sure you understand."

Nirimanye nodded, but held her aim, returning it steadily on Mouse's neck.

"I do, more than you can ever know." She said softly.

"Gentlemen, I'd like to assist you, but Griffon is under my protection." Sir Hugh said with a soft tone of danger aimed at Mouse and his boys. "As my squire, I am his master, no other man can claim his life or deliver punishments for any crime he commits." Sir Hugh reached down to a coin-filled purse at his hip and pulled it free.

"This will cover his debits, and you will trouble him no more." Hugh threw the purse over at Mouse who caught it deftly and grinned, he shook the heavy purse and his greedy eyes shone as he heard the clinking of the gold within.

"Thank you very much." He said as he put the purse in his pocket and took his feet off the table. He stood up and tipped his hat to Nirimanye who tracked him with the arrow as he moved. "Come on lads, our business is concluded here, sorry Barry, no dead man's boots for you tonight." He said as they moved to the door.

Mouse turned and tugged on his waistcoat. "Pleasure doin' business with ya Griffon! Call again if ya need some scratch!" he grinned Mouse turned and left the cottage as an arrow struck the doorframe near his head.

Sir Hugh walked up and shut the door behind them with a loud bang and yanked hard on the arrow, eventually pulling the shaft free of the head which remained embedded in the wood. He turned to Griffon.

"Now, you owe me. Your repayments will be taking your oath of service, undergoing your training and then taking the knighthood that is your Grandfather's legacy."

Griffon started to protest but Sir Hugh held up a hand.

"Griffon, this is not negotiable." Sir Hugh said. Griffon nodded his agreement, feeling trapped in a nightmare that never seemed to be ending.

Sir Hugh held his hand out to the lad.

"Men of honour shake on an agreement, Griffon." He said, and grinned when the young man took his offered hand firmly and hook it.

"Good, we have a lot to do."

Chapter Four.

Far to the north of the little farm near Hestow, beyond the safety of the borders of Vallonde, within the March of Darkness, a great migration moved, Centaurs again roamed lands that had been theirs millennia ago.

Beru, the most recent ruler from the Great line of Centaur kings, second of that name and so named in honour of his ancestor who almost ruled the world, but was banished to the other realm, now walked beside his sister, Sila. Her equine form was sleek and muscular like his, her human torso bore the scars of a warrior as did his. The breastplate armour that she wore was made of a toughened orc hide from one of their many wars that they had waged in their prison realm.

Two thousand years their ancestors had to prepare for the time that they would return to take that which was ripped form their grasp. Now their generation stood on the plains where the great battle had been waged and lost though magical means. Before too long, this land and the others beyond it would be theirs.

"I swear, my sister, I will break the royal bloodlines of each nation. Each man and woman, From the oldest to the babe in the cradle, will feel the steel of my blade, I will avenge the defeat that we suffered and take what our ancestors were denied." Beru said with a fire in his voice.

Sila nodded as she looked around the world that neither one had been born into, but that they had been told would be theirs one day should their seers prophecy prove true. Each generation that had gone before theirs had been raised to train for war, sometimes it came between each Centaur clan, other times between the Centaurs and their former allies.

In the other realm, Beru had brought the great clans together again, using the namesake of his ancestor to unite the clans after he defeated the leader of each opposing clan. From Orc, to Minotaur to Centaur and the lesser creatures. Each leader was beheaded and their clans brought under Beru's rule.

"Brother, the lands to the North, Mithorlas, are ours. Our ancestral home. Why can we not simply reclaim it and live as we are, go back to the old cities that our ancestors had built and rebuild our civilisation?" she asked. She would never outright tell him but she wanted a peaceful life, where she could find another mate and raise more children.

Her first mate had been slain in a war in the other realm. Her only son Tolm was all that she had left of her first husband. But she wanted a new life, a life like the one her old nurses had told her handed-down tales of. Where Centaur and man worked together. Before the ancestral wars that caused them to be magically banished from their home.

Beru had discounted them as silly tales for silly children when they were young and had gone out to train with his father's men, ever preparing for the war to come.

Sila had soon followed his lead, not wanting to incur her brother's wrathful anger, but always having the dream of peace in her heart and the back of her mind.

Beru turned on her with a snarl.

"Peace? The only peace we will have is when the people of the southern lands lie broken and bloodied at our feet, their bodies will go to feed the land and the fine crops that we will grow," he moved up in front of her, his body pushing hers back a few steps, she could see the rage in his eyes. "Do you not understand dear sister?" he said, the force of his words causing him to spit as he spoke.

"Of course I do brother, but why, why can we not seek peace with the peoples of the south?" she asked him.

Beru snarled again with malice and struck her hard with his open hand.

"You need to remember something." He said as he grabbed her wrist and pulled her along. They were not far from the place where it had all ended, and yet where it had all begun. He galloped down the valley, a firm grip on her wrist forcing her to run hard beside him. A stone statue stood rearing above a group of crumbled stones, a lone Centaur, the first Beru. His army behind him had turned to dust and rubble, but the great Centaur King still stood as perfectly formed as the day he was turned to stone.

"See him?" Beru said, pulling her in beside him and wrapping an arm tightly around her shoulders. He reached up and gripped her chin, forcing her to look up at the stone statue.

"That is not a carving of stone, my dear sister. That is our ancestor, Beru, for whom I am named." He released his sister and stepped proudly before the stone Centaur.

"It is for him I will reclaim what is ours, for him that I will take up our banners and standards and wage war on the South. In his name, and mine, I will claim the South and take my sword to the necks of the Kings and Queens of the Southern Kingdoms, and there is no force in this realm that can defeat me." He said, bringing a hand up to touch the clear crystal that was embedded in the equine chest of their ancestral Grandfather

"This, I vow to you, Beru the Black. I, Beru, of your line, of your blood, will take the lands of the South. The victory that was stolen from you, I will reclaim, and it will be bloody. The bodies of the enemy I will trample beneath my hooves, and their blood will nourish the lands that we will claim in victory." Beru knelt on his forelegs and looked up to the statue that once was his living, breathing ancestor.

Sila watched as her brother took a dagger from its' sheath and sliced into the palm of his hand, making a vow of blood to their ancestor. She lowered her head in reverence and knew that once on this path, a vow of blood could not be broken unless the one who made the vow was slain by his enemies.

Beru placed his bloodied palm over the crystal in his ancestor's chest and got to his feet. He turned and looked to his sister

"You will lead an army of my choosing, my sister, we will be victorious and you will rule a kingdom as a vassal queen to me." He said as he moved up to her, he reached up and placed his bloody palm against her cheek, caressing it and smearing his blood against the pale skin of her face.

Sila nodded. "It will be as you wish, brother, I stand with you on the battlefield, as always, and I will stand by you as a vassal." She said softy, bowing her head to her older brother, the stench of his blood rankled her nose and the wet sensation of it on her cheek turned sticky as it began to dry.

"As it should be, you will make a fine vassal queen, Sila, you are already a warrior, worthy of leading one of my armies, now that I finally have the Orcs, the Minotaurs and their allies at my feet, it is time to bring the rest of the filth of this world under my rule." He said as he turned and looked to the south.

"Come," he said returning his proud gaze to the north where their cities had lain empty for thousands of years. "First we reclaim our homelands form whatever scum has taken hold in our absence, then we will march on the south."

Sila nodded silently and followed her brother to re-join their people as they returned to their ancestral homes, guided only by the knowledge handed down to them from generations past.

***

In the little grove where his parents and grandparents had been buried, Griffon knelt by the fresh grave of his Grandfather. Nirimanye held a lantern, a cloak around her shoulders and a hood covering her head against the chill of the evening as stars shone overhead, their light twinkling through the overhead leaves of the trees above them. Two older graves lay covered with flowering daisy weed where Griffon's parents lay, His father died when he fell from a horse and struck his head on a rock when Griffon was but a babe in the crib, and his mother taken with a winter's fever when he was young.

The light from the lantern flickered over the headstones of the graves while the young man paid his respects to a Grandfather with whom he was often at odds with as a youth, finding the teachings that the old man had offered boring and archaic, in the impetuousness of youth, he did ot realise the value of the old man's words and lessons.

Six years of regrets flowed into his thoughts as he recalled the good times that he'd enjoyed with his Grandfather. Fishing with him as a boy in the little stream that ran down past the last pasture at the back of the farm, going into town on his birthday for a freshly baked sweet roll from the baker, covered in sweet baked custard and sticky with honey glaze where the custard hadn't dribbled down over the baked sweet dough. The warmth of his Grandfather's love and care when he had been sick, or when he had fallen and scraped a knee.

Griffon felt the warm hand of Sir Hugh on his shoulder.

"Let go of your regrets, Griffon, you must take your vow with a heart free of guilt, regret, anger and hurt." Sir Hugh said as he watched the young man at the graveside. Griffon nodded and sighed heavily, wishing that he could do as Sir Hugh advised, but struggling with the deepness of the pain that he held in his heart.

Nirimanye watched as Griffon looked up at Sir Hugh, regarding the handsome young man he had become when he had lost the gangly looks of his youth. She held her growing feelings for him deep within the walls of her heart, fearful that if he were to know how she felt about him, he might break it.

"I'm as ready as I ever will be..." he said to the Knight who stood before him.

"Very well," Sir Hugh said as he reached down and drew his sword, placing the point at the hollow at Griffon's throat he looked into the young man's eyes.

"Griffon, Son of Matias, Son of Ter, Direct descendant of Herimor the Warmage. Through virtue of bloodlines pure and strong, you are offered a place as a squire of the Knights of Erandia, then to take your final oath and be placed as a full knight. You will strive to find justice and bring it to those who have found none, you will serve the people of this world, and protect them from threats to this world along with your fellow knights and squires. Will you join us, with a pure heart, and with the courage to face the oncoming night?"

Sir Hugh looked into the troubled eyes of a man who might not be quite ready to take on the full weight of the oath that Sir Hugh was asking him to take, but Griffon nodded, the sharp tip of the sword scratching the skin of his throat, a small trickle of blood touched the tip of Sir Hugh's sword bloodying the sharp point.

"I... I will serve." He stammered, his voice trembling.

Sir Hugh put up the sword, sheathing it. "Very well, I take you as my Squire, tonight you will rest but you will be up before the sun with me and we will begin your training." He said as he reached out a hand and helped Griffon up to his feet.

"Before sunrise?" Griffon groaned not looking forward to the early hours that his new master was already demanding of him.

"Yes, and if you complain about it once more time I'll start your lessons right now." Sir Hugh threatened, Griffon closed a mouth ready to protest with a snap of teeth.

"Come along, Squire." Sir Hugh said as Nirimanye followed along, taking the lantern with her and leaving the little grove in consuming darkness.

***

Up in his old room, Griffon lay sleeping fitfully, taunted by nightmares.

He stood in a field alone, dressed in a heavy suit of armour while an army charged him from behind. The sound of horses greeted his ears and he turned, only to find that the army that charged him did not ride horses, they *were* horses, or to be more precise, they were Centaurs. Griffon turned and ran, while the Centaurs laughed at his cowardice, tears flowed down his face and he could smell blood.

As he ran he could hear the sounds of battle, he chanced a look over his shoulder and saw the Centaurs attacking the people he knew, Nirimanye drew her bow and fired arrow after arrow into the enemy only to be cut down by the lead Centaur, Sir Hugh was trampled beneath the sharp hooves of the charging herd. He stopped his face wet with tears as he watched the beasts destroy towns and cities, the people running for their lives to be captured in nets or slaughtered where they stood.

He felt helpless to stop them, and he stood still as they Centaur war host finally turned their attention to him, he turned to continue his desperate run but found himself facing the edge of a cliff, the bottom of which could not be seen for the distance to the bottom was unfathomable.

He felt hot breath on the side of his cheek and looked to see its source, the broad and angry face of the lead Centaur looked back at him.

"Are you ready?" it asked him.

"Ready…?" he said with a squeak.

"Yes, ready." It replied, shifting to his other ear to whisper the words in his opposite ear

"To…to do what?" he asked.

"To *WAKE UP!*" it roared.

***

"WAKE UP!" Sir Hugh shouted at him. By the gods he was a heavy sleeper.

Sir Hugh slapped Griffon on the cheek none too gently and the young man bolted upright, it was still dark, and the red tinge of the sunrise was on the horizon when he blinked sleepily trying to clear his eyes of the crusts of sleep that had accumulated in the scant few hours that he had managed to sleep.

"Ahh good you're awake, about time too. Get up, we have work to do." Sir Hugh said as he tossed a set of clothing at Griffon. Peasant rags.

"Can't I have decent clothing?" Griffon groused.

"Not unless you want to learn a little humility." Sir Hugh replied as he walked down the stairs.

Griffon groaned and flopped back down in the bed, putting an arm across his eyes.

The next thing he knew there was a bucket of cold water being thrown over him, he spluttered awake again.

"The next bucket will be filled with nightsoil. Now get up." Sir Hugh said sternly.

Griffon looked up at him in surprise, "Surely you wouldn't do that!" he said aghast.

"Want to try me lad? I've been waiting downstairs for you for almost forty minutes, you have two minutes to get dried, dressed and downstairs before I go and get my nightsoil bucket."

Griffon groaned and got up out of the soaking wet bed, shaking the droplets from his hair as he padded around to pick up the clothes from the floor where they shad slipped from the bed as he slept.

They were baggy and ragged, and itched in places. With hair still dripping from the dousing Sir Hugh gave him, he headed downstairs to the warm kitchen.

Sir Hugh was scrubbing the dishes that he had used for the porridge he'd made for breakfast, some still sat in the pot to the side of the fire. Griffon's stomach grumbled with hunger.

"Good morning, ready to start work?" he asked the young man in rags.

"After breakfast, yes." Griffon said as he sat down and waited to be served a bowl of steaming porridge. He turned to the stairs as Nirimanye walked down them in her simple work clothing. She smiled at the two men in the kitchen.

"Good Morning, Sir Hugh, Griffon." She said as she reached the bottom step. "Sleep well?"

"I did indeed my Lady." Sir Hugh said as he bowed slightly to her in deference.

"And you Griffon… I see you've already bathed." She said smiling sweetly, Sir Hugh handed her a bowl of porridge. She nodded her thanks and sat at the table and began to eat.

"Uh…" Griffon said, looking at the bowl of porridge and then looking to Sir Hugh with a question in his eyes 'where's mine?' Sir Hugh turned back to the dishes, wiping them dry with a cloth. Griffon sighed and got up out of his chair, grabbed a bowl off the shelf and moved to the pot to help himself to the porridge.

As soon as his hand touched the spoon to dip into the pot he felt a sharp slap on his hand.

"Ouch!" he yelped, dropping the spoon into the porridge and grabbing the injured hand. "Hey!" he looked up at Sir Hugh who was twirling the drying cloth into a tight rope and preparing to flick it at Griffon again.

"Tomorrow you will get up when I tell you to, then you can have breakfast. But for now…" He said as he flicked Griffon again with the cloth, but this time on his rump, causing him to yelp again and jump. "You and I will get started on the chores." Sir Hugh began to twirl the cloth again and Griffon eyed him warily.

"Okay! Okay!" Griffon said in a high pitched whiny voice as he alternately rubbed at his insulted hand and butt cheek.

"Good. Get started, go and milk the goat." Sir Hugh said, picking up a bucket and tossing it at him.

Nirimanye got to her feet, "I'll do that…" she finished the last spoonful of her porridge and quickly scrubbed the bowl and her spoon while Griffon watched, he handed her the bucket.

"My lady…" Sir Hugh said, stopping her with a gentle hand on her shoulder. "Griffon will do the chores today, you have done so much for Master Ter, please, have a day to yourself, for there will be much to do later when we start preparing for the Moot." He said as he gently took the bucket from her hands and shoved it back into Griffon's

62

chest. "And Griffon needs to learn the value of a hard day's work." He said glaring at the young man.

Griffon grunted with the force of the bucket hitting his chest, his hands automatically coming up to take it. "All right, all right, I'm going." He muttered as he stalked out to the sunrise-bathed yard in a huff.

The nanny goat bleated at him from the stall in the barn. Her strange eyes watching him suspiciously as he came around with the milking stool and the bucket.

"All right, you old bitch." He muttered as he settled down on the chair. "Let's get you milked." He set the bucket down under the goat's udders and reached with his cold hands for the bulging teats.

Cold hands met warm goat teats and the poor little Nanny bleated in shock. No sooner had Griffon started to pull on her udder did she start to kick and buck. A well-placed kick landing right on Griffon's groin, causing him to go down in a veritable array of swears and curses that would make a sailor blush and take a vow of silence for the rest of his days.

Griffon lay there waiting for the pain to ebb and the stars that danced merrily behind his tightly shut eyelids to go away and leave him in peace. The goat nudged him with her nose and bleated loudly in her ear before she began to nibble on the curls of hair on his head.

Nirimanye found him curled up in the foetal position.

"Oh, Griffon... Are you all right?" she asked him as she helped him up to a sitting position. He winced as his insulted balls shifted painfully.

"Yes... marvellous... absolutely marvellous." He said, his voice a few octaves higher than usual and strained through gritted teeth.

"You've never milked an animal before?" she asked him as she gently pulled on the Nanny's rope to bring her closer. Griffon watched through eyes half closed in pain, he watched as she settled herself on the stool and gently stroked the goat's neck and back, speaking softly to her, thanking her for her milk and telling her what a lovely girl she was. Griffon looked on in amazement as the goat placidly stood ready to be milked.

"This is how you milk her," She said, instructing Griffon, he watched as she rubbed her hands together to warm them and then placed the bucket beneath the goat's udders.

"You need warm hands, kind words and a gentle touch." Nirimanye leaned down and gently coaxed the milk from the goat, "Your turn, just talk to get gently, she will let you milk her." Nirimanye moved off the stool to let Griffon sit back where he started.

The Nanny turned her head and looked at him with trepidation, Griffon crooned gently to her, trying to soothe her little nervous tremors. He gently stroked the pelt of fur on her back as he calmed her shivers.

"Good, now warm your hands gently, rubbing them." Nirimanye said as she took both of Griffon's hands and pressed the palms together, pushing them to rub against each other and warming the skin of his palms and fingers with the friction.

"Now, gently ease the milk from the udders," she advised him. She watched, crouching beside Griffon as he pressed his hands around two udders and gently used his hands to bring the warm milk to squirt down into the bucket.

"That's it! You're getting it now." Nirimanye said with a smile and a gentle pat on his back as the bucket began to fill with creamy milk. Griffon smiled as he pulled gently on the udders, every so often the udder would squirt harder and splash his clothes. By the time the goat's udder was emptied of the morning's milk, he was covered in little splatters and stinking of cream and goat, but he saw the approval in Nirimanye's eyes and he felt a strange warm feeling in his chest.

Chapter Five.

Griffon sweated and cursed, a strip of sweat dampened cloth was all that separated his aching back from the harness of the plough. A whip cracked into the unfurrowed ground by his feet.

"Come on lad!" Sir Hugh said as he pushed on the plough "We need to get this done soon!"

"Then put the bloody horse in the harness!" he yelled. He had managed to pull the heavy plough and harness only a short way, his clothes were filthy with dirt and tattered from falling many times, his knees and hands were scratched and bleeding, but in the week that Sir Hugh had taken him to be his squire, he had not worked so hard in all his life.

"Not until you learn the lesson!" Sir Hugh said as he cracked the whip expertly landing the lash in the air just behind Griffon's ear.

"Hey!" Griffon said as he dodged the whip's lash. He threw the harness to the ground and stormed back to Sir Hugh who stood there laughing.

Griffon drew back and punched Sir Hugh on the jaw, dropping the laughing Knight.

"This is bloody insanity!" Griffon yelled, his face sweaty and red with exhaustion and anger.

Sir Hugh sat in the furrow that they had just cut into the earth and rubbed his chin.

"What was the lesson Griffon?" he asked form his seated position.

Griffon took stock and thought about it for a moment, all morning Sir Hugh had been riding him on his chores, telling him to do them in a way that made no sense but still achieved the end result, even though it took ten times as long to get them done. Many times Griffon had grumbled at the indignity of the work, and the bullying that Sir Hugh had started on him. Very slowly Griffon had become fed up with the treatment and the final straw was the crack of the whip right behind his now ringing ear.

"I'm not going to take any more of your fogging crap. You've been riding me all day and I'm sick of it. I can do the chores the right way or your stupid arse way." He stomped off towards the farmhouse.

"Where are you going?" Sir Hugh called out to him.

"To get the bloody horse and do this the right way!" Griffon said with a snarl.

"Griffon…" Sir Hugh called him back. "You learned the lesson." His master said from his place on the ground.

"You stood up for yourself against a bully, you decided to do things the right way. These are things that a Knight must remember to do, we often stand up for those who don't know how to do it for themselves, we teach the people to oppose their oppressors to seek a better way of doing things, not just an easy way but an honest way. The way I was forcing you to work was dishonest and harsh." Sir

67

Hugh said as he rubbed again at the bruise that was forming on his cheek.

"Now, some prisons in Beline actually do this to their prisoners as hard labour." Sir Hugh said as he looked up at Griffon. "They don't allow the prisoners to protest or fight back. There have been riots, the Belinese are a harsh people; they cut themselves off from the rest of the world after the war with the Elves, but that is not the point of this. You have learned the lesson and I hope you remember it when you become a Knight of Erandia, especially when you take your Grandfather's place as the High Master Knight."

Griffon nodded and smiled grimly, knowing that the lesson was one that had taken years to learn, from the time he was a young scrappy youth, leaving his Grandfather's home for the streets and finding that life was harder than it looked.

He smiled down at Sir Hugh, "I'll go get the horse." He said turning.

"Before you get the horse, Griffon, can you do something for me?" Sir Hugh said, causing Griffon to turn back.

"Sure." Griffon said.

"Help me up out of this hole, my arse is stuck."

Griffon began to laugh heartily, but reached out and pulled Sir Hugh to his feet.

Sir Hugh slapped griffon on the back. "Thanks Lad, now go get that horse so we can finish this field." He said grinning. Griffon nodded with a grin and turned back to get the horse. Sir Hugh watched him, the lad had made a remarkable transformation since starting his training

Muscle had started to come in and his features had gotten a harder edge to them with the work over the past few weeks. Each night he had fallen into his bed after Sir Hugh had finished with him and slept soundly, after two or three days of being woken up early by Sir Hugh, he had started to wake up at the required time by himself.

Any food that was placed before him at mealtimes were devoured heartily, fuel for his growing muscles. He had helped Nirimanye to sweep and clean the barracks under the cellar, and preparing to host the Knights and their squires.

Sir Hugh had gone to Hestone the fifth day after his arrival, after giving Griffon his tasks for the day. He had sent messages via pigeon to the forts, towns and cities where he knew his fellow Knights would be frequenting, or passing through. He had hopes that the first Knights might arrive soon.

But for now, he was busy preparing Griffon for his first training session.

"So, have you wrestled before Griffon?" Sir Hugh asked, as he leaned against the fence of the pigsty where the sows grunted happily and nosed through the swill in the trough.

"When I was a young lad, yeah. I'd tousle with my friends, I'd always win." He said boastfully.

"Well, that's nice." Sir Hugh mused. "Ever done it when it really mattered? Like when your life was in the balance?" he asked thoughtfully.

Griffon watched, his mouth opened to reply, as Sir Hugh opened the gate and let the two sows out into the yard to sniff out for mushrooms that grew beneath the trees. The happy grunting of the pigs distracted Griffon for a moment as they searched around the trees for mushrooms to devour, until he heard the scraping of wood on wood. He turned his attention to Sir Hugh.

"Right…" Sir Hugh said as he settled the pole from the fence across the length of the pigsty. "Think you can wrestle me off the pole and into the pig shit?"

"Absolutely." Griffon said with a grin.

"All right, here's the deal." Sir Hugh said as he approached the far end of the pole. "You push me off into the sty, and you get tomorrow off, you can sleep in do whatever you want and I'll do your chores." He said as he stepped up onto the pole, waiting for Griffon to do the same.

"If I win, you have to do all the chores, plus wash your filthy pig-shit encrusted clothes, cook the supper, sharpen all the swords in the armoury and shine my boots."

"And if we both fall?" Griffon said, wondering about the possibility of a stalemate.

"Then we both do the work together, and make it a half-day so we can rest." Sir Hugh offered.

Griffon thought about it for a moment, "Deal." He said as he got up onto the pole and steadied himself on it.

"Ready?" Sir Hugh said smiling.

"Are you ready to bathe in pig shit?" Griffon said cheekily.

"Only if you go in first!" Sir Hugh said as he moved quickly towards Griffon.

Hands connected with each other and muscles began to ripple and bulge as the two men strained against each other and gravity to keep from falling into a muddy, mucky mess. Nirimanye was drawing water from the well for washing, and came over to watch the two grunting, struggling men as they tried to wrestle the other off the pole, shouting encouragement to both.

Soon other voices joined in, shouting their encouragement as two Knights and their Squires joined Nirimanye at the fence. Griffon struggled hard against Sir Hugh but they were so evenly matched that one could not dislodge the other, despite the dirty tricks and attempts at knocking a foot from the pole to overbalance their opponent they threw at each other.

A chorus of catcalls and shouts joined in as more men appeared from the road, tired and dirty but enjoying the entertainment that they found at the pace of the Moot. Nirimanye laughed as Griffon pushed forward a little, making Sir Hugh slip a bit.

"Come on Hugh! Your little Squire is making you look like a fool!" one of the Knights shouted good naturedly.

71

"Pig shit is good for the complexion; why don't you dive right in lads!" another man laughed.

The thick pole began to wobble and roll as the two men leaned side to side to keep their balance, Sir Hugh hadn't secured it very well and the round pole rolled to the side as Griffon lost his balance, dragging Sir Hugh down into the stinking mud where the pigs loved to wallow. The mud was soft, and fouled by pig shit. They hit the mud with a sick squishing sound, their bodies and began to sink.

"Argh!" Griffon shouted and began to choke on the stink.

Sir Hugh floundered about, trying to find the solid ground in the mud, flinging bits of muck as he flailed his arms to the uproarious laughter of the several Knights and their Squires who had arrived in the short time of their wrestling match.

"Well met brothers!" Sir Hugh laughed as Griffon tried to get out of the muck, dry retching as he went. Sir Hugh scrambled over to his Squire and pulled his leg hard, dragging him back into the mud face first.

"This fine, upstanding mud man is my Squire, Griffon, the grandson of our departed Master Knight Ter, the inheritor of the Title, of the lands we camp on, and the Burden." Sir Hugh slapped Griffon on the back heartily and helped him up out of the mud.

"Isn't he the idiot who unleashed the Centaurs?" one of the knights asked. Sir Hugh scowled.

"What if he is?" he growled.

72

"And you want to give him a bloody medal? Let him lead us? The boy can't even hold his own against a pigsty."

"Think you can outdo his efforts?" sir Hugh said in challenge.

"By Beru's blue balls I can!" the knight said with a laugh as he unbuckled his armour and handed his weapons to his squire. "Hold these, boy I'll be but a minute!"

The log was reset and Griffon climbed atop it. "You can do this, Griffon, stand up to him, if you don't none of these men will follow you when the time comes." Griffon nodded and looked out to the gathering of Knights, more had arrived while they were resetting the log over the pig sty.

Griffon eyed the knight warily. He stood straight and took his time, while his opponent goaded him. Griffon took a deep breath and stepped forward on the wobbly log. The other knight wobbled a little on the unsteady log, Griffon placed his feet sideways to help with his balance.

"Here piggy, piggy, piggy..." the knight jeered, "Got some lovely muck for you to wallow in." Griffon raised his hands, his legs wobbling as much as Griffon's. with a sudden shift in his weight, Griffon swooped down in a crouch, kicking his left leg out and kicked the jeering knight's legs out from under him. The knight hit the log, his legs spread and his manhood instantly bruised. He whimpered and slid off the log into the filth below.

The crowd of knights laughed and cheered Griffon's victory and Sir Hugh took his hand to help him down while the other knights watched their fallen companion slowly drag his sorry self from the sty.

"Come lad, let's get cleaned up." He grinned through a face that was still covered in filth. They left the pigsty and turned towards the cottage.

"You dare step foot in that house and I'll have both your hides!" Nirimanye said, stepping before them, a broom clutched firmly in her hands. "Over to the well, the two of you, and wash yourselves down in the vegetable patch, the water and muck you wash off yourselves will be good for the garden." She advised, a small smile on her face.

"Thank you, my Lady, if you would be so kind as to play hostess for a short time while Griffon and I clean ourselves up, it would be greatly appreciated, and I would be more than happy to help you once I have cleaned up." Sir Hugh bowed, pulling Griffon into a curt bow with him.

"Of course." Nirimanye said smiling. She turned and ushered the Knights and squires into the cottage as Sir Hugh led Griffon, who still retched from the stench, the way to the well.

The strong hands of the Knight pulled up the larger bucket of water, drawing from the depths of the well. He handed the bucket to Griffon and nodded over to where the big vegetable garden was.

"Go on, it's going to be cold, but we can have a proper hot bath later." Sir Hugh said. Griffon took the bucket, sloshing water over his feet as he walked to the vegetable garden. He knelt down in the dirt, not caring anymore about getting any dirtier than he already was and began to strip off his shirt and pants, leaving his unders on.

A bucket of cold water was thrown over his back and he gasped in a lungful of air at the shock of it. Griffon turned to a grinning Sir Hugh.

"Bloody hell, that was cold!" Griffon said breathlessly, he picked up his larger bucket of water and threw the chilly water over Sir Hugh who laughed and tried to dodge but was hit hard by the water.

Nirimanye walked around the side of the barn with an armful of clean clothes for the men and found them playing like children trying to keep cool in the short but hot summer, both were saturated with streaks of mug and pig dung still on their bodies, spaces of skin flushed with the shock of the cold well water poked out as rivulets of water cleaned away the mud.

"When you two have quite finished, the Knights and Squires are awaiting you in the barracks." She said, startling them both. Griffon's hands flew to cover his crotch, despite the fact that he was wearing underwear, and his face flushed a bright crimson with embarrassment. Sir Hugh however simply bowed to Nirimanye.

"Thank you, My Lady." He smiled, Nirimanye grinned and put the clothing on a barrel that stood beside the wall of the barn and turned back to the farmhouse.

Griffon went and collected another two buckets of water and began to wash himself down.

"Sir Hugh," he asked, "Why do you call Nirimanye 'My Lady'?"

Sir Hugh was silent a moment, as if he was trying to think of the right thing to say, or he was searching for an answer that dodged another reason.

"Well… I was taught to be respectful to everyone, by my master. It's a trait I think that you should learn, in fact all knights are taught this. We serve the people so it's important to show some measure of respect to them." Sir Hugh said as he sluiced water over his back. Griffon came around wand poured the remains of Sir Hugh's bucket over him, rubbing down Sir Hugh's back to get the last of the dirt from his master's body.

"So I'm going to have to call every woman 'my Lady' and every man 'my Lord'?" Griffon asked, lifting his own bucket up and upending it over his head for a final rinse.

Sir Hugh nodded as he took up a rag and began to dry himself.

"That's correct, but not every man or woman deserves that honorific, some people of lower or meaner stations in life, like criminals just simply get a 'Sir' or 'Madam'." Sir Hugh replied as he tossed a drying rag to Griffon after he had dried himself and began to get dressed. He watched as Griffon dried himself and then tossed the young man's clothes to him.

"Bring in some wood for the fires downstairs when you are finished." Sir Hugh said as he put his and Griffon's clothes in the larger bucket and took them to the washing area for cleaning before he went into the house to the chorus of greetings by the men who had arrived.

Griffon watched him go and wondered at the turn of events in his life.

***

"So we have to get to the Kings of Beline and Vallonde and warn them of the coming war. We know the Iron Kingdom will help, you'd have a hard time keeping a Dwarf from a good battle, it's the one thing they love more after carousing and feasting." Sir Richard said as he sat back on one of the kitchen chairs with a mug of warm cider in his hand.

Griffon entered the little house with an armful of wood, the kitchen was filled with men as the conversation continued.

"What of the Elves? Their throne has stood empty since their last king was killed in exile almost a hundred years ago. They are a scattered people." Sir Francis said.

An earthenware mug shattered on the stone floor as Nirimanye's hand slipped at the washbasin.

"Excuse me..." she said softly as she quickly cleaned up the shattered pieces.

"I'll go clean those clothes, Sir Hugh." She said quietly, Griffon stopped her.

"I already took care of that, you don't need to worry about it... My Lady." He smiled, pleased that he had taken care of the disgusting chore of scrubbing his and Sir Hugh's clothes of the mud and pig filth.

"Oh… thank you." She said as she continued out the door, brushing past him as she went, there was a decidedly warm blush to her cheeks as she passed him.

"Nirimanye…?" Griffon called after her, confusion in his voice. He liked her, she was a kind and gentle woman and he wondered what it was that he had done to upset her.

"Leave her be, Lad. The Elves have had a hard time of it in the last hundred years." One of the Knights said from the table.

"Beline waged war on them for a good three hundred years, something about an arranged marriage gone sour with one of their Princesses and an Elven Prince, their Princess decided to run off with a guard and the Elves felt that their honour was insulted, the marriage would have strengthened the two nations, and brought them closer," The Knight said as he pulled out a pipe and began to tamp down some tobacco into the bowl.

"But instead the king of Beline decided to make war, he was wrong to do it and the Elves lost more than an ally, they lost their home. Their King and the Elven queen who was pregnant fled for the safety of her unborn child, this was just under a hundred years ago, before your time." Another Knight continued the story.

"We tried to mediate between the two but each time their negotiations broke down and they continued their war against each other. Now the Elves are scattered, The Queen was killed in exile by Belinese assassins, and the Heir went into hiding." Sir Hugh finished.

"So…" Griffon said softly, thinking, "We need to get the scattered Elves together, but how?"

"We need to find the Heir and convince them to take the empty throne." Sir Richard said.

"Easier said than done my brothers." Sir Thomas said after swallowing a mouthful of mead.

"Well… Maybe not. I may know where to find the Elvish heir. It was a secret kept so close that even the heir doesn't know his or her destiny." Sir Hugh said as he leaned against the wall, his arms crossed over his chest and hands holding just below his shoulders. His eyes were on the door that Nirimanye had gone through to the outside world.

***

A little way beyond the grove where Griffon's family lay buried and where he had taken his Oath of service, Nirimanye stood before a simple grave.

A handful of freshly picked wildflowers were clutched in her hands as tears fell from her tightly closed eyes. There was not much that she could recall of her mother's face, but Ter had told her often how much she looked like her, especially in his last years. She was just a little girl when her mother had brought her to the safety of Ter's home.

They had run from the Belinese assassins for as long as she could remember, and the relief that her mother showed at finally being in the safety of the Grand Master's home was evident in the memory of her mother falling to her knees in gratitude.

Ter had shaken his head and begged her mother to rise to her feet, helping her up as he did so. He had said it would be an honour to protect her and the daughter whom he hoped would one day bring the Elves back together.

"You have a hard road ahead of you, My Lady." Sir Hugh's voice carried softly on the wind to her.

She didn't turn around, but lowered herself to the ground, reaching out and placing the flowers on the grave of her mother.

"I do not know if I have the strength or courage to call my people to rally." She said with a voice that showed the emotional strain that she felt.

"We all walk a road laid out for us." Hugh said. "Sometimes there are obstacles that we have to either find a way around, leap over, or destroy completely." Sir Hugh said as he placed a hand on her shoulder.

"But there is only one of the blood alive today who can sit on the empty throne and send the call out to the Elves, as soon as you sit upon that throne, Every Elf will return home." Sir Hugh said as he knelt down beside her, his fingers brushing over the blades of grass at his fingertips.

"It will be a grand homecoming, and they will be glad for it, your people are shattered and broken, they need to find their way again. I know Ter has taught you well, now you need to take those lessons and use them to lead your people." Sir Hugh said softly. "There is a lot we must do in the meantime. I think it's necessary to go to Beline and see the King, he is young and idealistic. He might listen to reason as opposed to his late father, who was a stubborn old goat." Sir Hugh said as he got to his feet.

"Whenever you are ready, come back in. I'll see to the Knights; you just worry about what you need to do." Sir Hugh said as he turned and walked out of the smaller grove behind the graves of Ter and his family.

Chapter Six

Steel clashed against steel in the stabling yard of the farm. Several heavy horses grazed in the field beyond while men shouted encouragement and tips to the swordsmen who sweated and grunted in their heavy armour and wielded swords against each other.

"Bring your shield arm up Griffon!" Sir Hugh shouted at the last second, Griffon saw the strike and brought his arm up, his opponent didn't follow through but instead delivered a kick to his breastplate, sending Griffon staggering backwards to fall on his arse.

The sword of his opponent was at his throat as he lay sprawled on the ground.

"Yield?" his opponent said from behind his helmet. Griffon shifted and kicked his legs in a sweeping motion, knocking his opponent down in a clatter of armour beside him. He rolled over and onto his opponent and drew his dagger, with his free hand he knocked the helmet off his foe and placed the dagger at the throat of the young squire below him.

"Yield!" he ordered with a strong voice.

Below him his opponent nodded. "I yield, good fight Squire Griffon." Griffon got up off the fallen squire and helped him to his feet. Griffon nodded and clasped a gauntleted hand against the squire's elbow, with the breathless young man returning the gesture.

"Good work." Sir Hugh said as he came up to the two Squires. "But remember, it won't be so easy to knock a

Centaur off his feet, the best place to strike to bring one down is their equine chest, where their second heart is." Sir Hugh said, pointing to his own chest.

The sound of a horse galloping over the dirt road that lead up to the farmhouse caused the group of Knights and Squires to turn, a hooded rider sat astride a sweating and trembling chestnut horse, it was obvious that the animal had been ridden hard by the foam at its mouth and the harsh and heavy breathing through flared nostrils.

"Sir Hugh! I bring grave news, The Centaur Host has attacked the mines and forts of the Iron Kingdom. The Dwarven King has sent me as an envoy to seek your help and guidance." The rider said as he removed his hood and dismounted.

"Squire Collin, take the man's horse," Sir Hugh said to one of the squires.

"Come and rest and we will discuss the situation." Sir Hugh said as he turned to his men and nodded them to attend.

***

Beru's body was covered in blood as he galloped hard against the Dwarves that opposed his forces. The Orcish soldiers that ran beside him were similarly splattered, their mouths open, white and yellowing fangs bared as they breathed hard with the exertion of running beside the powerful Centaur King.

Blades rose and fell as Dwarves tried to fight to defend their mines, blood ran in rivulets along the small water drains that took out any water from the rock face that might have leaked through the walls.

Sila watched from a hill not far from the battlefield, her heart heavy, but her face impassive as she watched the battle below. Every so often, the wind would blow the stench of blood and death upwards to her position. She held her bow ready in case of a counter attack came from the dwarves, but she knew that would never come.

She smelled the arrival of the Orc general, Gashur before he was able to be seen.

"Victorious, my Lord Gashur?" she asked the bloodied warrior. He returned a grin and held up the severed head of a Dwarf.

"Their leader, a Dwarfish princeling… pathetic." He said with a snarling grin.

Sila watched as the Orc general used the Dwarf's long plaited hair to tie the severed head to his belt, there were three other severed Dwarf heads already tied to Gashur's leather belt. Their eyes were open, unseeing in death, and different expressions ranging from surprise to horror was their countenance in death. Blood trickled down the Orc's legs leaving bloody trails down to his feet as he walked.

"Then these mines are yours, as my brother has promised you. May your smiths create weapons of great power for our soldiers in the coming war." Sila said as she held her bow in her fist over her heart in salute.

84

"Your warriors are brave and strong, Lady Sila, I doubt your brother will have any trouble taking the pathetic creatures of the Southern Kingdoms. I don't know if they will make good slaves, but they may make good sport in the arenas."

"Perhaps they will." She said watching as the warriors returned from the battlefield. Some warriors remained to take any survivors and use them back in the mines as slave labour.

Beru came galloping up, bloodied and sweating. The bloodlust clear in his eyes as the adrenalin pumped through his body. His face one of pure victory as he grinned at his sister.

"Ahh, my darling Sila! We were victorious! Those Dwarven scum cowered and ran until they realised that we had them surrounded on all sides, even their little bolt holes were covered, then they fought like rats trying to escape a burning house."

"Where do we strike next, my brother?" Sila asked as she put away her bow.

"The Beline Kingdom, my scouts report they have split from the other wretched southerners, they have also scattered the Elven people to the winds, I am grateful to them for that, for the Elven nation stands with an empty throne, making the Elves weaker." Beru pulled a cloth from a bag and began to clean his sword of dwarf blood.

"We celebrate the victory this night my brother?" Sila asked.

"We leave as soon as we can my sister." Beru said as he shook his head. "We will only celebrate when our victory is total and the lands of the Southern Kingdoms are blessed with the blood of the dead." His sword cleaned, he re-sheathed it and turned to his camp-masters.

"Prepare to break camp, we will travel towards Beline's borders as soon as we have packed." Beru shouted.

His men scrambled to break down tents and extinguish fires while others worked to shackle the prisoners whom were being taken back to Mithorlas to be sold as slaves.

***

Nirimanye folded the last of the clothes and packed them tightly into the leather rucksacks. She looked around her room. For a very long time this place had been her home. Ter's home.

Now the house overflowed with Knights and their squires. Sir Hugh said there were more to come, as they were scattered to the four winds across their world and it would take time for those in the far reaches to arrive.

Sir Hugh decided to send a large group of Knights over to the Iron Kingdom to assist the Dwarves in preparation for more attacks, and the final inevitable war with the Centaurs. Others were directed to seek an audience with the King of Vallonde and warn them of the Centaur's return, and also to help them prepare.

Sir Hugh had also decided that the three of them would go to Beline themselves and try to convince the young king there to prepare for the war. She didn't know when she would be back but she knew that they would need to travel through Erellond, her abandoned homeland.

Nirimanye's hands shook. She was afraid of leaving the safety of the farm, but she was also excited about seeing lands that she hadn't seen in over eighty years. Despite her age she appeared to be a young woman in her early twenties, as was the way with all Elves, the long lived spent their childhood growing at the same rate as human children, but then when they reached adulthood their aging slowed down considerably.

A knock on the door startled her. She turned to face the noise. Griffon stood in the doorframe.

"Nirimanye, Sir Hugh is ready to leave, we have to get going." He said as he entered her room. "Have you got everything ready?" he asked her as he came up beside her.

"I think so." She said. "Oh, wait one thing." She went to the simple wooden dresser that stood against one wall and opened a drawer. She pulled out a little amulet that once belonged to her mother, who had given it to her on her deathbed. She placed it around her neck, remembering that her mother had told her it would keep her safe from harm. She sighed as she placed a hand over the round amulet, feeling the cool gold warming against her skin.

"I'm ready." She said as she nodded.

Griffon shouldered her rucksack and they left her room. Several knights and squires would remain here, making the little farm their base of operations with the extra room down in the cellar would house them and any other knights who might arrive while Sir Hugh was gone.

The trio left the farmhouse on horseback, Griffon was still unused to riding, but Nirimanye was as graceful as ever on the back of her horse.

They rode all day with little company, other than the odd passing merchant or traveller on the road. But there was an air of fear to the people that they passed. Word had spread of the attacks on the Dwarves, the sudden disappearance of the magic barrier that hung over the March of the Damned and the appearance of a great army of Orcs and Centaurs.

Where for thousands of years none had roamed, the Darklands were again inhabited by death and danger for anyone fool enough to roam the barren plains.

"Come on you two." Sir Hugh said after they had purchased some food from a travelling merchant and rested for a short time. "We won't reach the border with Erellond for a few days, we will seek shelter at Fort Fox, a little further down the road. If they deny us a safe place to rest, then we will camp at the stream by the fort." He said as he mounted his horse.

"Fort Fox, isn't that near the March of the Damned?" Nirimanye asked as she put foot to stirrup and mounted up.

"Yes, but we should be safe, I don't think the Centaurs will be in the March, not yet." Sir Hugh said as he urged his horse to a walk.

Griffon jumped a little trying to get into his saddle, only managing to get back in after a few tries as his legs were stiff and sore, and he had to get his horse up to a trot to catch up, his arse bouncing up and down painfully in the saddle.

"Isn't Fort Fox one of the Knight's Strongholds?" Griffon asked as he tried to slow his horse down, his efforts unsuccessful as he passed Sir Hugh and Nirimanye.

"Get control of your horse Griffon, or it will think it can control you!" Sir Hugh advised.

"I'm trying!" Griffon said as he tried to pull back on the reins. With his ungainly struggles to get control of the horse, he accidentally kicked the animal in the side, causing it to think he wanted it to gallop.

"Griffon!" Sir Hugh called out as the animal broke into a desperate gallop away from the group.

Nirimanye urged her horse to a gallop, chasing after Griffon's uncontrolled animal, Sir Hugh following on his own steed.

Griffon held on to the reins for dear life as his horse sped along the road, "Watch out! Clear the Way!" he shouted at the travellers on the road. An old man was at a crossroad that lead to one of the smaller hamlets, pushing a cart filled with cabbages. Griffon closed his eyes and prepared for the pain of the fall he knew was coming.

Instead he felt his horse leap into the air and over the cart, he heard the cry of the old man as he dove out of the way of the horse. He opened his eyes after he felt the jolt of the horse landing on the ground and continuing its' mad gallop, turning back to see Nirimanye's horse gracefully leap over the stopped cart and the old man shouting obscenities at them as they galloped away.

Sir Hugh had the good grace to ride his horse around the cart and the old man, but losing time in doing so as Nirimanye and Griffon's animals gained more ground away from him.

"Griffon!" Nirimanye shouted to him, the wind carrying half of her voice away. "Pull gently on the reins, take control of him!" she urged her horse to gallop a little faster, slowly gaining on Griffon's horse as he rode haphazardly, arms flapping as if he was ready to take off. She slowly got up beside him, she reached out and grasped at the flapping reins.

Her head was close enough to whisper soothing sounds to the horse, Griffon felt it slowing down, soon they were at a canter, His horse and Nirimanye's both cantered at an off timing to each other, and he felt a little motion sick as he watched Nirimanye's horse move in comparison to his own.

She got the horses to a trot and then finally a walk, where Griffon could feel his mount trembling and its breath heaving in its' chest.

"Thank you…" he said gratefully to Nirimanye.

She handed him back the reins, "You're welcome, walk him a little bit now to cool him down, you will both be tired later and you will be very sore."

"Ugh," Griffon said, grimacing as he reached down between his legs and adjusted his buised and battered manhood. "I already am sore." Nirimanye giggled at the look on his face.

"Don't laugh, it hurts almost as bad as when the goat kicked me in the balls!" Griffon said with a groan at the memory.

"Well you're going to have to get used to it, and come to an agreement with your horse on who controls whom." Sir Hugh said as he cantered his horse up to them. "Come on, we still have a way to go before we reach Fort Fox, and I'd like to be there before sundown without any more wild horse chases along the Hestone Road." He said as he moved his horse along the road at a stately walk.

They travelled down the road for a few more hours until the grey stone towers of Fort Fox came into view through the thick forest.

"There it is." Sir Hugh said pointing through the trees to the stately old fort, "Fort Fox, the watch point for the March of Darkness and Vallonde, there were other forts built at the crossing points in the other nations." Sir Hugh said as they continued along the road towards the fort.

Soldiers could be seen walking post on the Battlements under the bright flags of the Vallonde Royal House.

"And yes, Griffon, Fort Fox was once a Knight's stronghold, but a king of Vallonde requested to take the Fort's upkeep over a hundred years ago, and we never took it back, we just have a small group of Knights posted there, serving justice on the road to the travellers who request it."

"Don't the King's guards do that? The Constabulary?" Griffon asked as the gates of the fort drew close

"No, the King's guards serve the forts and the King's City, the Constabulary are for the townsfolk, there is often little justice out on the roads and in the wilderness, there are bandits and men of lawless natures who prowl the roads looking for easy marks." Sir Hugh said as he raised a hand to stop them.

"Hello the Gatekeeper!" Griffon called out to the bulwark above the portcullis of the fort.

"Who calls the Gatekeep?" a soldier shouted down from a small bulwark above the gate.

"Knight of Erandia Sir Hugh Aldwyk of Swaford travelling with Lady Nirimanye and Knight's Squire Griffon du Frain of Hestone request lodgings for the night!" he called up.

"Wait there!" the guard called down. They waited for a few minutes while the guard came down to open the portcullis.

"There is lodging available to the Knights and their guests, but there have been movements in the March of the Damned, the nightwatchmen are on alert." The guard said as he let the travellers in.

They stabled their horses and Sir Hugh left them in Griffon's care while the Guard sent for the commander of the fort.

Nirimanye collected her bags from the saddle and looked around, there was a nervous edge to the soldiers, they were wary and the feeling of something not quite right was high in the air, as if they were anticipating attack at any moment. She looked at Sir Hugh and could see that he too felt it.

"Something isn't right, there's a danger in the air here." He said softly, "Be ready to leave at a moment's notice." He turned to the Commander of the fort as he approached.

"Greetings Sir Hugh, Welcome to Fort Fox." The commander shook hands with the knight.

"Thank you commander, we just wish to stay for a night, and we will be gone before sunrise in the morning." Sir Hugh said as he looked up at the darkening sky. "Your Gatekeeper said that there had been movements in the March of the Damned?" Sir Hugh asked as the Commander ushered their little group inside when Griffon joined them.

"Yes, our lookouts reported movement down in the southern reaches, two riders, they approached the monument and then left, though the eyeglass that the lookout used had a crack in the lens, so he wasn't sure if they really were riders." The commander opened the door to a small room with four cots.

"Scouts reported seeing strange beasts as well, and then we got word this morning that the Dwarves have lost several mines to Orcs and Centaurs on the edge of the March. Now I've heard rumours of Centaurs returning after we lost the Lights of the Damned above the March, that's when the strange sightings began."

"Strange Sightings…" Sir Hugh said under his breath.

"Aye, things are not as stable as they once were. Dark times are coming; I can feel it in my bones." The Commander said as he nodded to Sir Hugh. "Mess hall is open to visitors, evening meals are being served now."

"Thank you, Commander. If there is anything we may do to help you, please let me know." Sir Hugh said, watching the commander go as he closed the door.

"Well," He said turning to his travelling companions, "Were there any doubt that you've released the Centaurs and their allies from two thousand years of imprisonment, Griffon my lad, it's all but gone now" Sir Hugh sat down on one of the cots, placing the heavy bag with the ancient tome on his lap. The top flap fell open, revealing the end of the dark book.

Griffon eyed the book warily as Nirimanye set about making the beds up for the night.

"It's not going to do any more harm, Griffon, but you are the only one who can read this, I need you to study it to find out how we put the bastards back in." Sir Hugh said as he patted the canvas cloth that made the bunk's base. "Sit."

Griffon moved uneasily to sit beside Sir Hugh.

"Now, go over it carefully, it is very important that you don't miss anything, and if you don't understand a

94

phrase ask me about it and I will try to help you to understand." Sir Hugh said as he hefted the book out of the bag and handed it into griffon's lap. The young man huffed with the weight of the book and gingerly opened it as if it were a venomous snake and might bite him.

"I'll go and get us some supper before the kitchens close." Nirimanye said as she finished with the other beds and swept out of the room.

Sir Hugh watched as Griffon read the old pages of the book.

"This passage here," He said pointing at words only he could understand "It says something about blood of four royal houses must be used to bind the evil to the other world. There is only one royal house in Vallonde, what do they mean by 'the blood of the four royal houses'?"

Sir Hugh thought for a moment, recalling his history training when he was but a young squire. "Back in the Darkland War, there was a great alliance between Man, Elf and Dwarf, two Kingdoms of Men, one of Dwarf and one of Elf., Where once four kingdoms stood, only three truly remain today, even though the borders of Erellond are recognised, the Kingdom of the elves does not have a king or queen to sit on its throne, thus it is a broken land. It is the four kings of the four realms that lie south of the Darklands that it refers to."

Griffon read on. "All was surely lost, until they found the last King, his blood spilled upon the ground, his heart beating its last. They bore their blood unto a crystal of pure clarity, until it stained with their lifeblood. The spell was cast when the Magus thrust the shard into the equine chest of Beru, and all his kind and the kinds of his armies were banished to the realms beyond the veil."

Sir Hugh nodded, "Yes, one of the kings of Men was slain in battle and they were able to get the last drops of his blood as his heart stopped beating. With this kind of spell, a Blood Bond, the blood givers must still be alive when their blood is given, otherwise the crystal will fracture and the spell will be reversed." He explained.

"So if the king had been dead when they took the blood from him?" Griffon asked, not sure if he liked the answer.

"Then we would be the ones who were banished. Keep reading." He said, urging Griffon.

"Thus was cast the greatest spell in the realms, ne'er to be cast again lest the Gods of magic take offense." Griffon finished. "Well, that's not good... I don't want to piss off the Gods of magic..." he sighed and turned the page to continue reading. "I can't read this..." he said, looking at the strange script on the pages.

"What?" Sir Hugh said stunned, his eyes swept over the pages, "Its' in High Tallendic, the language of Elven Royalty." He flipped through a few pages and found another change in the script. "And this is in Hodlgren-dar, the language of the ancient Dwarves." Sir Hugh said in awe, "This must have been written by the old kings themselves." He said with reverence.

Nirimanye returned carrying a tray with bowls of stew for each and a small bread roll.

"This is interesting indeed," Sir Hugh said softly, pouring over the ancient scripts.

"Any luck?" Nirimanye asked as she handed out the stew.

"There might be something you may be able to help us with, My Lady." Sir Hugh said, looking up earnestly into the lady's face.

"Oh?" Nirimanye asked.

"Yes…" Sir Hugh said as he offered the book to her, opened to the Elven script.

Chapter Seven.

Grunts and snorts were muffled as the raiding party moved closer to the fort, their soldiers were on alert, but many of them had just eaten, and with full stomachs they were in a lull.

The Orc leader moved swiftly. His goblin and imp troops scampered up the high walls of the fort, the weather-worn stone no hindrance to their sharp claws. They quickly slit the throats of the guardsmen who walked the walls. No alarms sounded, not even as the smallest of the invaders hauled up the portcullis and allowed his allies to enter.

***

Sir Hugh sat up in the darkness. Something was very wrong. He drew his sword and went to Griffon's side, he shook the boy to a near-woken state, only to have the lazy sod grumble something about lessons and roll over to go back to sleep. Sir Hugh kicked out the legs of the cot from underneath Griffon's slumbering body and the bed collapsed to the cold floor with a grunting cry.

Sir Hugh clamped a hand over Griffon's mouth before he could utter a sharp and seething curse at being woken up so rudely.

"Sword ready, lad." Sir Hugh said to the young man. Griffon was on his feet and scrambling for his sword in seconds. Nirimanye sat up, a small dagger in hand, she leaned down and pulled her pack out from under her bed. She laid the dagger to the side and pulled out a long canvas wrapped package, she silently unwrapped it to reveal a beautiful hunting bow, with care and speed she strung the deadly weapon and collected a few arrows.

Sir Hugh watched in the dim light that was cast from the crescent moon into their small room by the tiny window, and knew that his companions were ready for whatever had tickled his internal alarms.

He moved to open the door when loud bells started to clang from the courtyard.

"Enemies in the fort! To Arms! To Arms!" the shout was roused and called throughout the keep, the sounds of booted feet scrabbling to their places to meet the enemy was heard muffled on the other side of their door.

"Stay here, do not open the door for anyone," He said, his eyes wide in the pale moonlight. "Griffon, I charge you with Nirimanye's protection, do *not* let her fall." He said placing a hand on Griffon's shoulder.

"But…" Griffon started to protest, but Sir Hugh put up a hand silencing him.

"When I go, bar the door with cots, chairs, whatever is in the room, I'll knock three times, then four then three, which is how you will know it is me." Sir Hugh said as he quickly donned his armour as the bells continued to ring. He opened the door cautiously and watched as more soldiers ran past, their chainmail clinking as they ran, some still buckling their scabbards to their belts. Sir Hugh slipped out of the room and shut the door.

He moved into the flow of soldiers as they ran towards the battle, but only after he heard his two charges shifting the cots and other meagre furniture to stack against the door. As he jogged along he asked one of the men what was going on.

"Fey, Milord, Orcs, goblins and the like, bastards managed to get in somehow!" the soldier said as they ran to the battle.

Sir Hugh and the soldiers burst out into the chill of the night to a flurry of shouts, grunts and the clashing sounds of sword against shield. Sir Hugh drew his blade and worked muscles that he had only recalled were there during his training sessions with Griffon, his body had lost much of its fat in the time he had taken Griffon on as squire, and his body revelled in the fight.

A Goblin's head rolled across the field of battle, getting kicked as men and fey beast moved about, each trying to gain the upper hand over the other. Sir Hugh hacked and slashed at a scarred Orc, his snarl dying on his ugly face as Sir Hugh stabbed him deeply in the chest.

The stench of blood of the Fey and of man joined the atmosphere and a in the chill of the night, a light fog formed, hugging the ground where the bodies of the dead lay cooling.

A few miles away from Fort Fox, another group of warriors moved silently through the March of the Damned. Sila led the men who were sworn to her brother's service across plains that had not seen such death and destruction since the banishment of their ancestors two thousand years ago. They crossed over the border into the abandoned elven lands and moved quickly into the night, their number uncountable as the fog descended on them.

***

One of the Guards poked at the severed head of an Orc with the toe of his boot. Snarling yellow teeth and blood red eyes frozen in death stared back at the young soldier. Men moved about clearing the dead, which included the commander of the fort.

"Well, this is a right bloody mess now." The young soldier remarked.

"You have anyone who can replace the Commander? One of the older guards perhaps until the king brings in a new commander." Sir Hugh asked and then advised the young soldier.

"All o' us here are new recruits Sir, Fort Fox is a training fort, has been for a while now." The young soldier said, admitting his inexperience, his body shook with the battle shock. "Ne'er seen so much blood." He mumbled. Sir Hugh placed a steady hand on the boy's shoulder.

"You will see more and soon if we do not stop the threat from the north." He turned and walked back to the keep to return to Griffon and Nirimanye.

Griffon heard the signal of knocking and practically threw the furniture away from the door to clear it.

"What happened?" he asked when he opened the door, looking aghast at Sir Hugh's bloodied armour and sword, dripping crimson blood on the flagstone floor.

"The Northern armies of the Centaur host sent us a little raiding party of Orcs, Goblins and Imps." Sir Hugh said as he righted one of the tossed about cots and sat down on it. He cast about for his pack and pointed at it, Griffon got the hint and grabbed it, bringing it to the Knight. Sir Hugh pulled out an old shirt and proceeded to wipe what blood that had not dried on the armour off onto the cloth.

"What... what does this mean for our mission? Do they know we are here?" Griffon asked, his eyes wide in fear.

Sir Hugh sighed heavily as he cleaned his armour "It means that we might have company on the road, and they might not be too pleasant, but then dealing with the King of Beline isn't going to be pleasant either, but it will be necessary."

Sir Hugh looked up at Griffon, knowing that he hadn't answered the second question. "To my knowledge, they don't know of us so that might be to our advantage. There's no sense to this raid, there was only a small party of raiders and it was more like it was designed to keep us focused on their attack, something's setting some old wounds to itch and that's usually a sign of more trouble brewing."

"When do we leave?" Griffon asked.

'In the morning," Sir Hugh said tiredly as he removed his armour and lay back down exhausted from the short but hard battle. He lay an arm over his eyes.

"Shouldn't we leave soon as possible?" Griffon asked as Nirimanye went to collect the heavy cots from where Griffon had scattered them.

"No," Sir Hugh replied, "I just want to rest my eyes for a while and we will leave fresh, I don't think there will be another attack tonight." He shifted himself into a more comfortable position on the cot and rolled to his side. Soft snoring issuing from his mouth shortly after. Griffon looked at Nirimanye in the dim candlelight, she shrugged and went back to her righted cot to finish off her interrupted sleep.

Griffon watched over the two of them sleep. However, it was not coming for him any time soon. He picked up Sir Hugh's discarded armour and went in search of cleaning cloths and set to work cleaning the Master Knight's armour and sword. He looked exhausted the next morning when Sir Hugh and Nirimanye awoke.

"A Soldier gets sleep where he can, Griffon." Sir Hugh admonished the lad. "But I thank you for cleaning my sword and armour, I commend you on your initiative."

Griffon looked back at him with red-rimmed bleary eyes and nodded as he gathered his things and prepared to leave the fort.

***

Griffon's horse chomped at its bit as it trotted through the green forests of Erellond. Nirimanye was extremely quiet and tense as they passed through the borders. Her eyes searching every piece of the land as they passed and if Sir Hugh noticed the Elven maiden's discomfort he said nothing.

They had passed through the town of Lastowe the day before and spent the evening in a rough inn where most of the townsfolk seemed to congregate for loud drinking and carousing sessions through the evening. Sir Hugh had smiled and slapped Griffon on the back telling him to enjoy himself, despite the lad's gloomy countenance. Little sleep was had that night, and awoke late the next morning, their heads heavy with hangovers.

After travelling for almost the entire day, they arrived at a small abandoned Elven town. Sir Hugh moved them quickly through riding closely beside Nirimanye as they went through the eerily quiet town.

Not far out of town, they approached a fork in the old road. Nirimanye guided her horse, taking the road to the left instead of the right before she urged her horse into a hard gallop.

"Niri…" Griffon called to her, but she spurred her horse onward down the poorly maintained road.

Sir Hugh looked at Griffon and then kicked his own mount to a gallop to chase the wayward Elven lass. Griffon looked on in shock, Nirimanye had never acted like this before.

He watched as the two riders moved to the distance, then realised that he probably should be chasing after them, or he'd get leftbehind and alone on the unfamiliar roads. He kicked his horse into a gallop, chasing after them.

Overhanging branches whipped at Nirimanye's face, stinging the skin and making her eyes water, something called to her on the left fork of the road, she felt it pulse in her veins, compelling her, drawing her inexplicably to one place.

She left the road for a small overgrown trail, her horse changing its' gait to a trot to get through the thick scrub. She continued on for a short while before she stopped.

Hidden within the forest there was an old castle built of a pure white stone that seemed to ignore thenormal stains that came with the passing of time. The remains of the small town that surrounded it had started to be reclaimed by nature, with Vines and trees growing where once Elven society had flourished.

She pushed her way through the overgrown vegetation and moved to the Castle proper.

Sir Hugh pushed his horse through the overgrown trail, finally finding the town and the castle. Nirimanye's horse cropped grass nearby he cast about for her but there was no sign of her.

"Nirimanye!" he shouted out but got no response. He called again is voice echoing through the white marble halls that were invaded by vines of ivy and grasses that fought for life in the patches of light that shone through the filthy windows, but again nothing. Sir Hugh dismounted and began to move through the little town, he noticed her trail leading up to the Castle and with no hesitations, he plunged into the darkness of the Castle's entrance.

He found her in the throne room, a hand on the white and gold marble throne, her head bowed and her brows furrowed as a shaft of daylight shone directly upon her, as if it was the Gods themselves who had chosen her for this great and powerful burden, and not her blood right to reclaim the throne of the Elves.

"Did you not know of your heritage, Your Majesty?" Sir Hugh asked her.

She sank to her knees with a soft sob. Sir Hugh went to her, putting an arm around her shoulder.

"No... But I suspected I might have been nobility." She said with a heavy sob. "My mother... I was very young when she died, and Grand Master Knight Ter took us in shortly before she was poisoned by the Belinese assassins who were after us. She told me I was special, but I thought that it was something that all parents told their young ones."

Sir Hugh nodded, "It was at the request of your parents that we, the Knights kept your heritage a secret. But we knew that should you come to your homelands, you would be drawn to this place, to know who you are, and that you are the rightful heir to the throne of Erellond, your people will return to the kingdom, should you but sit on the throne and call to them, they will come."

"And Erellond will be whole again?" she asked him.

Sir Hugh nodded. "Your people will go through many trials, this war with the returned armies of the North is

106

but one of them." He looked up at the throne. "But it is up to you to decide if you should take it now, or upon our return from Beline. He placed a hand on the arm of the marble throne. "I would suggest that we travel to Beline first, your throne will still be here, and we will have a better idea on where the Belinese King stands, if he is with us, or if he stands alone."

Griffin came puffing and shuffling noisily in to the throne room. He whistled softly at the beautiful room, its columns of white marble flushed with veins of gold as his eyes adjusted to the different light. "This place is amazing, isn't it?" he asked as he ran his hand over the creeper-covered marble.

"This is the throne room of the Royal house of Ellynwold, you stand in the city of the same name. Ellynwold was once the seat of power and the capital city of the Elven nation, its throne stands empty, waiting for its lost heir to reclaim it." Sir Hugh said softly as he looked at Nirimanye who knelt on the floor, her hand firm on the chill stone of the throne's base.

Griffon looked from one to the other and then walked up to the dais on which the throne was set. "Will they ever find their lost heir?" he asked as he looked at the throne, he boldly turned and placed his arse on the worn cushion.

Sir Hugh took the four steps up to the throne and grabbed Griffon by the scruff of his neck. He unceremoniously threw him out of the throne's seat and onto the leaf and dirt covered floor. Griffon landed heavily with a whoosh of air from his lungs as his stomach smacked into the hard marble tiles

"You have no right or claim to this throne, Griffon, it shames me to see you sit on it with such audacity, as if it is your right! There is only one here who has the right to claim it." Sir Hugh said with anger vibrant in his words.

His voice echoed along the halls, startling a small flock of sparrows that flew through the throne room and out a broken window above the throne, with the last bird in the flock managing to drop a dollop of warm shit on Griffon's cheek as it fluttered over him with frantic beats of its' little wings.

Nirimanye looked at the small speck of white as it dribbled down Griffon's cheek. He scrunched his face up in disgust and wiped at his face. Nirimanye covered her mouth with a hand and giggled, her eyes showing their mirth. Sir Hugh sighed and walked up to her, he offered her his hand with a smile, helping her to her feet.

"My lady." He said softly to her as she stood and brushed the dirt from her riding dress. "Your people will follow you to the ends of time, you know this. We will not push you to take the throne until you are ready, and the Knights will stand behind you." He said, bringing her hand up his lips to kiss her knuckles.

"I know, and I thank the Knights for their support." Nirimanye said softly, "But I will take the Throne when we know that we can stand safely, without Beline trying to destroy us again for I know we won't survive their wrath a second time." She said as she moved to the Throne, running a hand over its smooth marble surface and returning the worn cushion to its place in the seat.

Sir Hugh watched her. "Come let's go." He said as he took her hand in his and led her down the dais.

Griffon stayed on the floor. Scowling at something. "What is that?" he asked, and pointed at an object that lay on the floor, a shaft of light catching the golden end of it. He pushed himself to his feet and walked with a slight limp over to the item.

"It's a bow." He said as he pulled it out from under a creeper, He held it in the light and brushed the dust from the bow. The string had been broken but the weapon was still serviceable, even after a hundred years of disuse.

Sir Hugh moved up beside him, leaving Nirimanye on the dais. "That is…" he looked over the weapon and then to Nirimanye, "Valladorn… The Bow of the King."

Nirimanye looked at the weapon in Sir Hugh's hands, he approached her and presented the weapon.

"My Lady," he began "this bow was your father's, and by the right of your heritage, it is now yours. May it serve you well." He said with reverence as Nirimanye placed a hand on the bow and lifted it from the upturned palms of Sir Hugh.

Griffon looked at the two. "What… wait…" he said lifting his hands up, palms out in a stopping gesture. "So, if the Elven King who died a hundred years ago was your father… then that makes you…"

"Griffon, you've obviously not worked it out yet, Nirimanye is the Queen of Erellond, and *she* is the lost heir to the throne of the Elves, the rightful Queen to sit upon the

109

throne." Sir Hugh said as Nirimanye looked modestly at the two men.

Chapter Eight

"But... but... you cleaned chamber pots, scrubbed cooking pots and ploughed fields..." Griffon said as he moved closer to his travelling companions.

"Nirimanye and her mother were given sanctuary by the Knights of Erandia. She was not yet born when her father was slain in this very room, his body was taken by the Belinese and no-one knew what had become of it." He looked at Nirimanye who was enchanted with the beautiful bow, but he could tell she was listening by the tears that gathered in the corner of her eyes.

"She died a few years after I was born, I think I was six?" she said thinking hard,

"Yes, and Ter was about forty by then I think but you were still a little girl, and you still are a young one by your people's standards."

"My Grandfather was over one hundred years old when he died?" Griffon asked with awe. Sir Hugh looked to him.

"Boy, you don't know much about your bloodlines do you?" Sir Hugh asked. When Griffon shook his head, Sir Hugh sighed. "You've got the blood of the long lived running through you. Your Grandfather was one-sixteenth elf, though he looked completely human, he and his father both lived to be over a hundred and twenty years old, though he only had your father as his child, and he had already gone on and married your mother by the time Nirimanye had come under his protection."

"So, I might live to my Grandfather's age?" he asked Sir Hugh.

"You might, but only if you wise up a little bit." Sir Hugh said as he gave Griffon a swipe upside the head, shifting some of the young man's hair as he did.

"Come, we have to keep moving, the King of Beline awaits and those Centaurs and their Orcish friends won't wait at all." Sir Hugh turned on the ball of his foot, crunching dried grass and leaves under his feet. Griffon waited for Nirimanye to pass, with as courtly a bow as he could manage, he let her go before him before he fell in behind.

Nirimanye turned her head to regard him over her shoulder as she walked. "You don't have to treat me any different, Griffon, I'm not a queen yet." She said softly.

Sir Hugh smiled and spoke as they left the Castle. "My Lady, you are wrong in that regard. Whether you like it or not, you are the Queen of the Elves, you carry the Bow of your father, and the blood of your royal parents runs through the veins that lie beneath your skin. You are the rightful ruler of the lands of Erellond." He caught the reins of his horse and mounted up, waiting for the travelling companions to do the same.

Griffon tried to help Nirimanye into the saddle but she shooed him away. Sir Hugh chuckled at Griffon's crestfallen appearance.

"The Queen of the Elves has learned to live an independent life, Griffon, she relies on no-one, thanks to your Grandfather." Sir Hugh got his horse through the first part of the abandoned town with the others following behind. Soon they were back on the road to Beline.

***

Beru looked out over the small village that stood ten miles past the border of Beline with the Darklands. Children played in a field not too far from their lines while their mothers worked washing through the small stream, oblivious to the warriors who waited patiently.

"Take the young, they will make reasonable slaves, females as well, we can give them to the Orcs to sport with after the battles to come." He said to one of his men. The Centaur soldier nodded and went to prepare the nets and cages for their captives.

Beru watched as his men snuck up slowly to the happy scene, Sila had come this far and had waited for her brother to arrive with a larger force, now he felt the bloody anticipation rising in his chest with each beat of his human and equine hearts. His fingers curled around his sword and he knew that soon, the people of this town, this country of Beline would know that the Centaurs had returned.

He moved quietly and lowered his sword swiftly in a signal to attack.

His men surged forward in a line of powerful equine bodies with a roar, startling the women and children as they worked and played. Screams of fright rose through the sun-lit field as the Centaurs ran down women and children, while others in their lines took off towards the town.

Beru chased a blonde woman through the waters of the stream, her face contorted in fear and her face streaked with tears as she ran. The water weighed down her dress as she splashed through, Beru following quickly after. The woman stumbled and fell into the water as Beru rode over her, his sharp hooves slicing through the thin homespun dress and into her flesh. His weight smashing bone and leaving her face down to drown in the water that was rapidly turning red with the blood of the woman and of that of others who had shared a similar fate.

Beru breathed hard as he looked at the corpse floating down the stream, he turned his attention to the village where coloured smoke started to billow up in several places and a bell began to toll. He snarled as he drew his sword and rushed out of the water to join his men while Sila and her troops captured the humans that still ran through the field, trying to find safety.

Within hours, the town had burned to the ground, the charred remains of the buildings still smouldered in places, and the men of the village lay dead, bloodied in the streets aor burned in their homes. Women and children were brought forward, bound in a line before Beru, many were injured and weary with fear.

Gashur came to stand beside Beru.

"An excellent capture, Lord Beru." He said with a grin, baring his large fangs.

Beru nodded, "Indeed, and I have a gift for you and your men for their loyalty, the females here are yours to use as you see fit, but the children will learn the slave's work of our camps." He said smiling, "Have your men separate the women from the children, and take which female you desire the most, my General." Beru indicated the line of shaking and crying wretches bound before them, and noticed Gashur's feral grin of lust as he spotted an auburn haired woman who cowered with the rest.

He marched up to her and grabbed her roughly by the arm, taking his dagger and cutting her from the lines. "This one will do nicely to warm my bed…" he said, grabbing her by the chin and forcing her to look at him. The woman whimpered in the hard grip of the Orc as Sila watched silently behind her brother. She kept her thoughts of disgust at the treatment of the females to herself. She wanted peace, but not like this, not through conquering, shedding of blood nor fear. She was in intelligent creature, but she knew that her own goals could not be achieved as long as her brother had the power.

Beru smiled as the other Orcs came and claimed a woman each. There was some fighting over the prettier ones, but soon the screams and cries of the women were heard through the camp as the Orcish warriors took them after the bloodlust of the battle.

Sila turned away from her brother's side and walked away. Beru watched her go as the screams began in earnest behind him, the children wept as they were taken to cages where the slave masters waited with whips to get the able bodied children to learn their places quickly.

Sila walked through to the fields where part of her brother's army was settling in for the night. Many of her men saluted her. She had proven herself in battle many times in their imprisonment in the other realm against other enemies that had claimed that realm. Their wars had been long and bloody, and finally, before their release and return to their home realm, they had ruled the other realm.

She came to the edge of the stream and looked down as something bumped against her foreleg. The body of the blonde woman who had been trampled by Beru had been stopped by a submerged branch. Sila had seen the woman cradling a small child before the attack and wondered at the fate of her own son.

Tolm was still too young to be in the war camps and was safely back at the capital in Mithorlas, though the plucky young Centaur idolised his uncle and had begged him to allow him to travel with them, Sila had told her brother in no uncertain terms that the boy was not to set foot on the battlefield, and she was grateful that Beru had agreed. The boy was all that she had of her mate, Torlan who had perished in one of the last battles before their return to the home realm.

She sighed and dislodged the corpse of the woman to float back into the stream, soon it would join the others in the river from which the stream was born. A warning for those who lived downriver that death awaited them.

***

Nirimanye splashed water over her face as in the stream. The water was cool on her skin and she opened her closed eyes. Sir Hugh and Griffon had set up a camp not too far from the river and the road and were preparing a simple meal of rations, dried meat, seeds and nuts and trail bread. Nirimanye looked down at something that had caught her eye, she leaned closer and looked into the pale and broken face of a blonde-haired human woman.

She scrambled back, screaming in fright. The heavy feet of Griffon and Sir Hugh pounded through to the river bank.

"My Lady?" Sir Hugh asked. "Are you injured." He said as he held the shaking elf in his arms.

Griffon looked to the river and cursed. There were five bodies floating in the river, caught by tree branches or rocks that lay just beneath the surface. Each one had been in the water for a while, and had bloated with gasses.

"Sir Hugh, where does this river come from?" Griffon asked as the bodies continued to float along.

"There's a town upriver, about twenty miles from here." Sir Hugh said. "Possibly a bandit attack, but..." he said as he knelt by one of the stranded bodies. "These are hoof marks, and horses are not common in Beline, their lowlands are too marshy." He left Nirimanye's side and gingerly touched the battered and bruised body, little semi-circular cuts in the flesh indicated where the hooves had sliced sharply against the woman's tender skin.

117

"You think that this might have been an attack by the Centaurs?" Griffon asked as he looked down at the body of the woman that Sir Hugh searched.

"Possible, but I can't be sure." Sir Hugh stood and wiped his hands on his cloak. "I think we should still camp here tonight, they will move downriver soon, we will probably pass them before they get to the next town, depending on how fast the river moves further south." He took Nirimanye's hand and led her back to their camp.

"I'll take the first watch, Griffon you take the next." He said as they reached the camp. Their horses cropped the sparse grass in their hobbled state nearby and the flames of the fire were starting to die down. Griffon put more wood to the fire and settled down beside it to rest while Nirimanye sat and stared at the flames.

Sir Hugh came and sat beside her, his sword loose in its scabbard ready to draw at a moment's notice

"You have seen death before, my lady, this is just part of war, another kind of death." He said softly as Griffon's snores started softly.

"You said it could have been a bandit attack..." Nirimanye said as she wrapped her arms around her up drawn knees.

Sir Hugh shook his head. "No, it was the Centaurs. A horse would have been lighter, the body of a Centaur is quite heavy. They are strongly built creatures, two hearts beat in the body, one in the equine chest and another in the human chest. I've been taught that the only certain way to kill a Centaur is to cut both hearts from the chest, or take the head." He said over the gradual crescendo of Griffon's snores.

"Then they have already started to invade Beline." Nirimanye said softly. "Let's hope that the King of Beline will listen to reason and join us in an alliance as our ancestors did two thousand years ago." She said softly as she lay down beside Sir Hugh. He took up her horse blanket and covered her with it against the chill of the evening.

"Try to sleep, we have another day's journey before we reach Kingsgate." Sir Hugh said as Nirimanye watched him move to the entry to the camp to stand guard.

Chapter Nine

King Dalon of Beline sat upon his throne and regarded the trio of travellers before him. Each looked weary from their travels, and each had a look of determination on their faces... well all perhaps except for the younger man, who seemed to be a bit unsure of himself.

The Knight of Erandia, Sir Hugh looked grim.

"So, your majesty, we come seeking an alliance with you in preparation for the armies of the north." He Knight finished.

The King sighed against his knuckles as they rested against the side of his chin. He was quite bored, and a good tournament would surely lighten his spirits.

"You say my people have already been attacked, Sir Knight?" the King asked.

Sir Hugh nodded, "Yes, your majesty, I believe that the bodies that we found were indeed that of the village to the north near the border of the Darklands." Sir Hugh looked tense.

"And according to your tale, this young fellow is the fool who unleashed their wrath on our world?"

"Yes, your majesty, Griffon did not know what he was doing." Sir Hugh said softly, keeping his eyes downcast at the king's feet.

"Hmph!" the king snorted. "And you lass, what is an elven whore doing with these two vagabonds?" the King said with a smirk. "Keeping their bedrolls warm at night are we?"

Griffon shook with anger. "She is the Heiress to the Elven Throne." He said with no restraint to the anger he felt at the king's disrespectful and disinterested "Queen Nirimanye of Erellond!" Sir Hugh snapped a sharp look at Griffon.

"Griffon!" he said warningly, but the damage had been done, the light in the King's eyes had already sparked.

"Queen of the Elves you say, lad?" the King stood from his throne, his cloak floating out around his body. He raised a hand with fingers filled with golden jewelled rings and pointed at the group. "Guards! Seize them and take them to the dungeons." Sir Hugh looked at the guards as they approached, he quickly got to the front of Nirimanye as Griffon got to her back, but they knew they were outnumbered even as they drew their swords to protect her.

"Lay down your weapons, please..." Nirimanye begged them. Griffon looked at her.

"Nirimanye... are you sure? He will kill you." He said softly, his sword still raised.

"I agree..." Sir Hugh said quietly.

"I disagree." The King said as he stepped closer. "In fact, I have a proposal for the Queen of the Elves." He said with a smile, "but one I will discuss with her, in private."

Sir Hugh looked warily at the king as he looked at Nirimanye with a calculating gaze.

"Lower your weapons…" Nirimanye said again, her voice slightly begging.

"I don't like this, my lady." Sir Hugh said as he sheathed his sword, he waited until he heard Griffon's own blade drive home in its' scabbard before he settled his own blade fully in his scabbard.

The King offered his hand to Nirimanye, "Come my dear, let us speak of this proposal." He said smiling like he had won the war already, Sir Hugh wondered if he was thinking of the new war, or the old war that had continued on between Beline and the Elves for years.

Nirimanye timidly moved out from the two men who protected her and took the hand of the king. He led her out of the throne room and in to a small area where there were soft chairs. The King's guards chose the moment that the door closed on the King and Nirimanye to take them.

Sir Hugh and Griffon were disarmed and placed in irons before they were hauled down to the dungeons. They were forced into separate cells and chained to the cold stone walls. Griffon looked over to the cell across from his where a skeleton grinned eternally at him.

Hours or days passed. Time was strange in the old dungeon, but finally the clatter of guardsmen echoed down the old stone walls. The guards stopped before the two cells and their prisoners. The King of Beline stood smiling.

"Well, this has been quite an eventful evening…" he said with a smirk. "Release them" he said to his guards, his eyes not leaving Sir Hugh's face. "My dear Lady Nirimanye would have you released, I however would have you kept in there, for I think you may have brought about our doom with your idiocy boy."

The guards entered the cell and unlocked their shackles, Griffon and Sir Hugh both rubbed their sore wrists as they were released.

"Your Majesty, Griffon did not know what he was doing when he read the book, where is it?" Sir Hugh asked.

"Oh. I had it burned Sir Hugh." The King said smugly. Griffon's shoulders slumped and Sir Hugh felt rage burning deep in his gut.

"My Lord… your Majesty, that book was…" Sir Hugh started but was interrupted by the king.

"Was the cause of all this trouble in the first place, if your Knights had destroyed it in the first place, then perhaps you might have avoided this disaster, as of now, you are expelled from Beline." The King said with a growl. "Your horses and gear will be returned to you on your departure from the castle."

"Where is Nirimanye?" Griffon asked.

"My Lady Nirimanye will be staying here with me, I must keep my bride safe from the enemy." He said, placing his hands behind his back.

"Your bride?" Griffon said, spluttering at the shock of the revelation.

"Yes, in exchange for the cessation of hostilities between my people and hers, and also for my vow of alliance with Vallonde and the Iron Kingdom against the Centaur threat, I have asked her to take vows of matrimony with me, she will bear me an heir and Erellond and Beline will become one nation, ruled by our offspring." The King seemed quite pleased with his deal.

"And she has asked for your release as a wedding gift." He said as he turned and walked away. Griffon and Sir Hugh watched the king depart as they stepped out of the cells and were escorted out another way. When they were alone, Griffon gripped Sir Hugh's arm.

"We can't leave here without Nirimanye!" he said hissing his words under his breath.

"We have no choice, Griffon," Sir Hugh said softly, taking the lad's hand from his arm. "She has made a sacrifice to ensure that we will have Beline's support and alliance in the coming war, she has also secured the safety of her people who will become Belinese citizens once she weds the king." Sir Hugh strode quickly down to where their bags had been placed.

"She can't wed him until she has taken her crown on the empty throne of the Elves." Sir Hugh said thoughtfully. He turned to Griffon, "We will see her again." He said as he checked through his pack and found the Bow of the Elven Kings, he revealed the bow to Griffon then quickly covered it up in the bag when one of the guards arrived to escort them out of the castle.

"So what do we do now?" Griffon said once they were back on the road.

"I will send word back to the knights by pigeon, we will converge on the old Kingdom of Erellond, bringing as many of the Queen's subjects as we can find, some knights will remain in their places in the halls of the Iron Kingdom and Vallonde as we have much still to plan with the coming war, we need to gather intelligence."

Griffon nodded. "Anything I can do, just ask." He said. Sir Hugh had noticed the steel in the boy's spine had grown stronger now that he had lost Nirimanye, Sir Hugh wondered at the lad's thoughts on the matter, but felt it best to leave it be.

"I will, now we'd best be gone from the city and this land, else we will end up in the king's dungeons again and I don't like being chained to one spot for any amount of time." Griffon nodded at Sir Hugh's suggestion and they rode out of the city as quickly as their horses were able.

***

From a richly appointed room, Nirimanye stood watching out the window as her friends rode out of the courtyard and into the city. Four maids awaited her, pouring hot water in to a large tub for her bath.

"My Lady?" one ventured closer to the Elven Queen. "His Majesty dislikes tardiness, and we must prepare you for the evening." The maid said softly. Nirimanye nodded, her forehead gently touching the cold glass once before she pushed herself away, leaving a hand print on the clear window. She turned to the maids and began to disrobe for her bath.

***

Sila strode into the darkened atmosphere of her brother's pavilion. Two human children stood to the side in rags with metal collars around their necks. She gave them a cursory glance before she looked to her brother.

"You summoned me, brother?" she asked with steel in her voice, she'd taken no slaves for herself in their attacks against Beline, Vallonde and the Iron Kingdom, wishing no part in the ownership of another being.

"I did, I have a surprise for you, a gift you might say." He smiled sweetly, Sila looked at his face, searching for the threat that she knew was hidden behind his joyful smile.

"And what gift could you give me that would tear me from training my men?" she asked as she took up a cloth and wiped the sweat that beaded on her skin exposed by her armour

"Your Son." Beru said, smiling as he shifted to reveal with a gesture, the young Centaur clad in royal armour and bearing a sword at his human hip.

"Mother!" Tolm said with obvious joy in his eyes.

"Tolm, my son," Sila said softly as she leaned down to capture his human upper body in a strong embrace. "What are you doing here?" she said, as she pulled back away from

126

him gently and caressed his young face. The boy was not more than twelve summers, and much too young to be in battle. Sila looked up at Beru as Tolm spoke happily

"Uncle Beru sent for me, he said I should learn to be a warrior like him!" the young one said excitedly.

"Did he now?" she said softly, eye flicking up to bore into her brother with annoyance.

"Yes! I'm going to be a great warrior like my father and my uncle, mother!"

Beru smiled at the boy's boasts.

"Your mother is an exceptional warrior as well, Tolm." He said as he came up beside the boy and placed a hand on his young shoulder. "Tolm will be training with me and he will serve in my ranks with my men." He smiled at the boy's jubilant grin.

"I won't let you down, uncle, I will slay many enemies and take many slaves for the glory of Mithorlas and her King!" the young Centaurs hooves pranced on the earthen floor of the tent in excitement.

Beru placed a hand on the boy's head and rubbed hie hair affectionately "Well you will need a better sword than that toy, but you need to work up to it." He said as he gripped Tolm's wrist and bade the boy bulge his biceps, "You need to work out a little more, but you are ready to start your training though. Go to the master of recruits and tell him you are to start training immediately!"

Tolm's face lit up with anticipation "Yes Sir!" he said and almost galloped out of the tent,

"Now if all my soldiers were as eager as that young man was to follow my orders…" he said pointedly at Sila who glowered at him.

"Why is he here? You promised me he would not be sent to the front lines. In fact, you told me he was safe back at home." she said as she rounded don her brother.

"And you promised me your unrelenting support, yet all I hear is you moaning about peace to your men, Sila if I did not know better I would say you were a coward, and a traitor." Beru said with a snarl. His hands moved fast to grasp her hand that would have stuck him across the face.

"Do not think that I am a coward brother, how many enemies have I slain in your name? How many races did we obliterate together? I lost my mate in one of your wars and still I stand by you, why?" she looked deep into his eyes and he saw the fury of a protective mother behind their brown blaze.

"Because I am the sister of the King of Centaurs, it is my duty to serve my king. But that boy…" she said, wresting her hands from his grip. "is not ready to die for his country, he is not ready to die for his king. He is not ready to die."

"Or his mother is not ready to face the reality that he is ready to serve his country, his king and himself." Beru countered as he gently reached up and stroked the face of his sister.

"You will see, my dear Sila, that he will serve and he will survive, his Dam and Sire's blood run strongly through him, he will be a strong warrior." He took his sister into his arms, holding on tighter than he should have for a simple, loving embrace.

"And if his mother should falter..." he said tightening his grip on her body. "I will slay him myself." He said, whispering the last threat into her hair. He felt her shiver with rage and could taste her fear in the air. "But if she serves me and my armies well," he said releasing her from his embrace but closing his hands painfully tight over her shoulders, "Then the boy has nothing to fear, for his enemies will fear him as they do me."

He pushed his sister away. "I will take care of him, Sila, and I say again, as long as you serve me, he will live, perhaps he will even rule after me."

Sila turned around and strode past the two cowering children.

"Sila!" Beru called after her, agitation in his voice. She stopped but did not turn to face him.

"It is right to offer proper obeisance to your king before you are dismissed." He said with a tone of danger to his voice. Sila turned sharply, her tail swishing through the air. She looked at her brother with anger evident in her eyes before she lowered them and bowed from the waist before she turned back to the entry to the pavilion and walked stiffly through.

Beru smiled to himself and ordered one of the two slaves to attend him as the shadow of his sister left the pavilion. As he watched her leave, his thoughts turned to his childhood, how his mother showed Sila more affection than she did to him, how their father would beam with pride when Sila hit the archery targets faster than anyone else. He had hated her for the love that his parents showed her. Now, he was King, he would order her on the most dangerous skirmishes, into the bloodiest battles. Sila would not survive this war.

Chapter Ten

Sir Hugh and Griffon had worked together to clear as much of the ivy and debris from the throne room of the Elven Capital. The call had gone out to the other knights and soon there was a small group of them working to clear out the dirt and debris from the old castle in preparation of the return of the Heir to the throne.

Many Elves had arrived to a bittersweet homecoming of their lands, long abandoned from the war with Beline, several of the elders fell to their knees and wept at the sight of homes long remembered, young Elves watched with wide eyes at the marvel of their city as it was revealed to them for the first time. Griffon had watched as the Elves went to work on clearing the streets of the fallen trees and quickly repairing their homes to a fit state to live in.

Sir Hugh had told him that many of the people who were returning to their traditional homes had been homeless in other lands, beggars, servants, some even having to resort to theft for survival, despite their being a people of the land, they did not do well in human cities.

A scout had been posted at the old road that lead to the elven capital, waiting for the arrival of the Heir and her betrothed, and a blast of a horn signalled their arrival at the outskirts of the Elven City.

Nirimanye rode on a white stallion, a dark blue riding dress adorned her body, the skirts drawn over the hindquarters of the horse and a soft look of sadness mixed with fear and hope across her face. The Elven people lined the streets to welcome the Queen to her lands, she rode before the King of Beline, but his eyes were on the city and the tales of riches that it held were undoubtedly running through his mind.

Sir Hugh looked at the lady as she passed, Griffon scowled at the king, but was brought down to a stiff bow by Sir Hugh.

"Don't aggravate him boy." He said his voice a harsh whisper, "Nirimanye needs the support of all the Knights and the squires as well as her friends." Sir Hugh said as the royal procession continued on.

"Can we see her?" Griffon asked.

"Soon, you and I are taking posts as her guards until the Royal Elven Guard is reinstated." Sir Hugh said as they rose from their bow.

"Good." Griffon said softly, his eyes boring holes into the back of the arrogant young King's head as he moved deeper into the city with the procession.

Nirimanye stood in the royal apartments, her attendants began to undress her while King Dalon lounged in a rough chair.

"Your city is quite lovely, my lady." He said as he sipped from a goblet of wine handed to him by a serving girl. "I'm glad my father and Grandfather never destroyed it completely." He said as his hand gently caressed the backside of the serving girl who stood beside him, the girl flinched, the decanter of wine twitching in her hand.

Nirmanye didn't miss the king's move against the serving girl and the girl's reaction, she said nothing.

"Forgive me, my lord, but we must prepare the Queen for the Coronation." One of the maids said as she turned to the king and curtsied. Dalon sniffed and nodded for the serving girl to accompany him with the wine.

"Very well." He said, his eyes on the figure of his bride-to-be as the maids began to undress the elven woman. When the doors had closed on the scene of what he considered his greatest acquisition, his hands moved quickly to caress and grope the serving girl.

He ushered the hapless girl down the corridors until he found a small alcove out of the way. The girl whimpered as the king pushed her in and pulled the skirts of her dress up.

***

Sir Hugh spoke softly with Griffon as they walked the corridors towards their post at Nirimanye's rooms. Griffon stopped as he heard something echoing down the corridor.

"Did you hear that?" he asked as they stopped to listen. A whimpering cry of distress caused them to move quickly towards the sound, their swords half drawn as they ran towards the woman's cries.

Sir Hugh stopped and drew his sword fully from its scabbard, Griffon a half second later.

"Unhand her!" Sir Hugh said, his voice so dark and menacing that it surprised Griffon. The assailant turned around, his face filled with lust and anger.

"You dare interfere with my sport?" King Dalon said still holding on to the serving maid by her wrist. Dalon had torn her clothes torn from her shoulders, she tried desperately with her free hand to cover her breasts.

"I dare interfere with a rape, Your Majesty. This is not the behaviour that a king should indulge in." Sir Hugh said as he levelled the sword at the king's neck. "As a Knight or Erandia it is my duty to stop injustices where I see them, be they done my noble or serf, king or peasant, all will be judged for their injustices against others; and this, Your Majesty is an injustice. No king should use his power or his position to take advantage of another in this manner." The King looked livid as Sir Hugh kept the sword at his throat. "Now release the girl, and I will let you leave with your honour intact, lest her Majresty, Queen Nirimanye discover this indiscretion." Sir Hugh ordered.

King Dalon snarled and pushed the maid towards Sir Hugh before he tucked himself back in his breeches and stalked away. The Maid broke down in Sir Hugh's arms and griffon watched as the king stalked away.

"We're just letting him go?" Griffon asked angrily as Sir Hugh put his cloak around the girl's shoulders.

"For now." Sir Hugh said sourly. "I do not like it, but he may be vital to the success of the war, and when this is all over, I'll kill him myself." Sir Hugh moved the girl gently into Griffon's protective arms. "Take her back to the servant's quarters see that she is cared for, I'll go take our post by the Queen's rooms, come back to your post when she is safe." Sir Hugh turned towards the direction of the Queen's apartments and strode out his anger.

Griffon looked at the trembling and weeping woman, "Come, My Lady, I apologise for the way you have been treated this day. Let me escort you safely to the servant's quarters where you may rest and recover. I will speak to the Steward and see if we can keep you away from the King of Beline for a while." Griffon said as he offered his hand to the young maid. She looked up at him with deep blue eyes, red rimmed from crying and she nodded.

"Thank you, good Sir Knight, may your life be blessed with love and honour." She said softly. Griffon moved quickly with her down the hall to the servant's quarters and returned to his post opposite Sir Hugh.

***

Tolm looked out over the battlefield, his uncle, King Beru watched the young man as he watched the massacre of dwarves and humans unfold beneath their position.

"To the south, there, you see?" Beru said as he leaned down and spoke softly in the boy's ear. "The cowards of the south prepare siege engines, the fools think that they can use siege engines against a mobile army, The Minotaurs and the Giants will overrun them in moments, crushing their pathetic machines underfoot, just watch." The bloodlust shone in Beru's eyes as the battle raged on, he could feel the young Centaur tremble with excitement, the flanks of his creamy hide shivered with each scream and clang of sword against shield that rose on the wind to their position.

"Soon, my boy, you will be down there, wreaking havoc and taking the heads off the shoulders of the enemy, you might even amass a nice collection, like Lord Gashur."

"Oh, of human women, my Lord?" Tolm asked looking up at his uncle with wonder, what use would a Centaur have for a human woman? They were not compatible. Tolm frowned as Beru laughed.

"No, boy, Heads, human heads." Beru clapped the young warrior on the shoulder and tightened his own armour. "Now you stay up here, I will show you how to force an enemy to surrender." He said as he drew his great sword and ensured his helm was on tight.

Beru galloped hard down the hill to the battlefield trampling over fallen bodies as he ran the gauntlet of fighters, his eyes on one of the humans as he fought. King Galrond of Vallonde swung his battle axe around to lop the head off a minotaur as Beru came up to him, his hooves skidding in the bloodied mud that had been churned underfoot.

The Centaur king rose up on his hind legs and struck out with his strong forelegs, hitting the Vallonde king in the temple, and knocking his helm from his head. Beru watched as the human king fell to the ground, dazed from the blow. "Surrender, or look upon your body from your severed head for the last seconds of your miserable life!"

Galrond scowled at Beru and spat on the Centaur, the spittle dribbling down his enemy's human chest, down his equine chest to drip down to the bloodied ground below.

"Then so be it, when I march on your city, its walls will fall, I will stand triumphant in your throne room and I will offer your daughters to Gashur, the lord of the Orcs for his playthings!" Beru swung his sword and felt the strong steel bite into the king's neck, he smiled as the king's head bounced once then rolled through the battlefield to be kicked around by soldiers as they fought to keep their stances in battle with their enemies and the sucking, bloodied mud at their feet.

Upon seeing the King's headless body fall, many of his soldiers fell to their knees in supplication to the enemy, others fought on with determination and soon their bodies joined that of the King of Vallonde. As the fight died down, Tolm ran onto the battlefield, crimson blood splattering up onto his equine stomach staining the creamy coat of his underside as he cantered towards his bloodied uncle as he smiled.

"Uncle, you were amazing, when can I prove myself to you in battle?" he asked, his eyes shining brightly with admiration.

"We will see how the next battle goes, or perhaps you may go deeper into this land and do some reconnaissance?" he smiled.

Tolm grinned broadly, excited for any chance to prove to his uncle that he was a warrior. "Yes sir!" the boy said, saluting with a fist to his chest.

"Very well, I have a plan in mind for you my boy, let us go and wash the stink of the enemy from our bodies, and celebrate this victory, then plan your mission." Beru placed a blood soaked hand on Tolm's shoulder, leaving a large, bloody handprint on the young Centaur's back.

***

Nirimanye looked at the tense faces of her friends.

"What is it?" she asked Sir Hugh, he shook his head, not budging.

"It is not your concern, not yet, my lady." He said, trying to assure her.

"Griffon?" She asked of her mentor's grandson and her dear friend. He looked grim, almost as if he was ready to strike someone with his anger.

"Something has occurred here; would you kindly tell me what?" She asked as she put her hands on her hips, making herself look even more beautiful in the distorted colours of the sun as they shone through the stained glass windows recently cleaned and repaired by the returning Elves.

One of the elven servants entered with a knock at the door.

"My lady, your people await." He said with a reverent bow.

Nirimanye nodded, "Very well, let's go. I suppose the throne has waited long enough for my bottom to sit upon it." She said as she gathered the skirts of her dress about her and moved out of the room. "And when all this is done, you will be telling me what has happened to make you both so grim and tight-lipped." She said with a meaningful glance at both Sir Hugh and Griffon.

Silver trimmed banners of deep blue fluttered from the ceiling of the royal galleries to the cleaned marble floors of the throne room proper. Elves, Humans and Dwarves in their finery waited in the recently repaired castle for the entry of the Heiress of the empty throne of Erellond. Everyone knew that after today, the empty throne would be empty no longer.

The Elves watched, enraptured by the elven queen's beauty. Men, women, Elves and Dwarves watched as she ascended the dais to her throne. New cushions had replaced the poor old ones that had been sun damaged, limp and threadbare, their new, blue satin covers shone in the flickering candlelight of the candelabras which stood tall behind and beside the throne.

Nirimanye stopped at the top of the Dais and went to bended knee before the throne, paying respects to those who had sat upon it before her. She rose and turned to face the crowd behind her. Her voice reverberated off the back of the royal chamber as she spoke.

"My Lords, Ladies, People of Erellond, distinguished guests, Lords and Ladies of the other great realms of Erandia, I ask you to bear witness to the restoration of Erellond, for today, I take my rightful place upon the throne, as determined by my bloodlines, and given to me by the grace of the Gods." She stood slowly and looked over the crowd. Sir Hugh stood to one side of the dais and Griffon stood to the other. Knights of Erandia were set amongst the people to ensure that there were no assassins within the castle or the throne room, sharp eyes searched for any untoward movements to the Queen.

"I take my place as Queen in a time where we approach a great war with enemies thought long forgotten. Let us join together in alliance to ensure that our world of Erandia is a peaceful place once again. I pledge my life and that of any of my children to be borne to the service of Erellond and her people, to the nations of Erandia in peaceful resolution of any and all conflicts that we might have had in the past, let us make peace with each other." She said.

She went back to her knees, shifting the skirts of the dress so she would not tear it when she arose again as Sir Hugh stepped up to the Dais with the elven crown in hand, a simple circlet with a blue sapphire set in the crest. Griffon approached from the other side, as King Dalon watched with a glower in his eyes from the gathered nobility.

Griffon took one side of the crown and Sir Hugh held the other.

"I Sir Hugh, standing Master Knight of the Knights of Erandia, do ask that you, Nirimanye, daughter of Aleron, daughter of Adrel, of the royal house of Erellond take upon yourself the burden of rulership of the lands that are yours by right of blood." He said, his voice carrying over the crowd of people in the hall.

"Will you Rule with peace and kindness?" Sir Hugh asked.

"I will ensure it is so." Nirimanye replied.

"Will you actively care for your people?" He continued

"I will walk amongst my people; no request will go without consideration." She said with a strong voice.

"Will you protect your people with sword and defend them with shield, should it prove necessary?" Sir Hugh asked, the crown still raised in his and Griffon's hands.

"I will protect those that are under my protection, and defend them with my very life." She said with a slight tremor in her voice.

"Will you take this burden?" Sir Hugh spoke loudly, his voice echoing through the halls.

"I will take this burden gladly." Nirimanye said. Sir Hugh nodded to Griffon slightly and together they lowered the crown onto her head.

"Then rise, Nirimanye, first of that name, Queen of Erellond, your throne is no longer empty." Sir Hugh said as he stepped back, nodding to Griffon to do the same. Nirimanye got to her feet to the applause of the gathered crowd. She stepped back a few steps, facing her people and the visiting dignitaries as she sat down on the throne. Griffon and Sir Hugh took their places by the Throne, serving as her protectors as the elven nobility, that which remained, came to offer their pledges of loyalty.

141

Nirimanye nodded and took the hand of each, accepting their pledges of service until every Elven noble had sworn their service to the Elven crown and its' queen. She motioned for Sir Hugh to approach the throne.

"Your Majesty, I Sir Hugh of the Knights of Erandia pledge our service to the people of Erellond, along with that of all other peoples of the nations within Erandia." He said as he knelt before the throne. "If you should need us, you simply need to ask. I will, with your permission, place a post of Knights and squires here for the purposes of fulfilling our duties as described in our code."

Nirimanye smiled warmly at Sir Hugh. "I thank you and the knights for your pledge of service to the people of Erandia, I fear we may need your wisdom in the coming days of this war from the Darklands, already they have attacked the Iron Kingdom, and Beline, we must ensure that they do not gain more lands and destroy us." She said as she looked up to the people.

"But for now, let us celebrate the restoration of Erellond. We have time for a little fun. Let the music play and the feast begin!" she said as Sir Hugh took his position by her side again. King Dalon moved quickly to take her hand with a smile that turned Griffon's insides sour, he shot a look at Sir Hugh that told him exactly what he thought of the lecherous king.

Music swirled through the halls as the celebrations of the restoration of a throne empty for a hundred years continued on through the night.

The predawn mists swirled around the silent invaders as they moved quickly through the woods, blades drawn as they approached one of the smaller forts. Hooved feet crunched softly over fallen leaves. Torches burned on the walls of the fort, no movement bar the flickering flames caught the eyes of the invaders. One of the soldiers raised a fist and drew it down, giving the signal to attack. They burst forth from the tree line to attack the small fort in Erellond.

The signal of attack went up as a bright fire flared to life in the signal tower, the light distinctively blue as pure alcohol was thrown on the flames to change the colour, the flames intensified with the new fuel and rose above the stone tiles of the tower's roof, the attendants running along the walkways to safety.

Tolm watched as the soldiers of the fort ran out to attack them, his Minotaur guards were the first to fall, their battle lust overpowering their duty to protect the young Centaur. He ran with them, his sword drawn, but his inexperience in battle almost cost him his life within minutes. As he ran towards the enemy, he was knocked over by a giant and almost trampled.

He looked up at the battle form his position and struggled to get up, his blade stuck in the earth not too far from him, the giant had bent it as it had trodden on it in its' haste to attack. From behind them a flood of enemy soldiers emerged from their hiding spots. Tolm's fear overrode his own small excitement of battle and he cowered as the enemy soldiers attacked his men.

His uncle would be furious with disappointment, there was good authority that the King of Beline was here while the Elven queen was finishing her first duties to the newly restored throne before he would take her in marriage. They were to attack here and kill the King of Beline so that his military knowledge would not be of any use to the enemy, and it appeared as though they had failed, by sheer numbers alone they had failed.

Tolm looked up as a giant pulled a large boulder from the ground and hurled it at the castle walls, the boulder sailed through the air effortlessly and smashed through the top part of the wall, smashing through the men who stood there. Cries went up from the wall, words carrying on the wind over the bloodcurdling cries of agony between combatants as the enemy ran forward and attacked the giant. Men screamed as they were flung away from the beast. He was finally felled when a brave solder ran up and slashed the giant's Achilles' tendon then the other.

The creature collapsed in a pain filled grunt to the ground, falling upon one hapless soldier who didn't get out of the way in time, his cries were cut as he was crushed by the heavy beast. The soldiers moved quickly to take the head of the giant from its' shoulders.

"The King! The king is slain!" the cries went through the battlefield like wildfire and the enemy stepped up their defence, soon Tolm managed to get to his feet, his coat stained green, brown and red with grass, mud and blood from the battlefield. He limped over to his bent sword and looked at it, dumbfounded, the weapon was useless.

A sword was at the boy's neck in moments, followed by others as he saw the dead and dying men of his mission laying upon the ground.

"Sir Richard, we have one alive!" the soldier called to a bloodied human as he approached.

"Hobble, bind him and bring him within the walls!" the Knight said as he wiped his bloodied blade clean on the cloth breeches of a Minotaur. Tolm was roughly handled and bound, his feet were locked in hobbles and he was forced along into the fort.

Within the walls, men ran around working to pull bodies from the rubble of the wall where the boulder hand landed. Simple cloth covered three bodies, but the hand of one man was sticking out from under the boulder, his hand was bejewelled with rings and men worked to push the boulder from the bodies it had crushed.

Tolm looked upon the outstretched hand of the King of Beline and sighed. He was now a prisoner of the enemy. He did not know how long he would live in their care.

He was taken down to the dungeons and put in the largest cell. The Knight brought him food and water and watched the young Centaur from the other side of the bars.

"What were your orders, soldier?" he asked sternly as he pulled a chair up and settled himself down on it.

"Why should I tell you, Human? Soon my uncle the King of Centaurs will raze this castle to the ground and your men will adorn the trees as a warning to any and all who pass here that the Centaurs are supreme." He said with a bravery that he didn't feel, his tail flicked with nerves.

"You are young for a warrior, untried." The Knight said thoughtfully. "Let's see, you dropped your sword after you didn't run fast enough to keep with your line, and it got trampled by a Giant, one of your own allies, and you didn't think to pick up a sword of a fallen soldier. Yes, you are untried young one." The Knight smiled.

"My uncle the great King Beru will come for me, and you will all be slain at his hand!" Tolm shouted, his voice high pitched with fear and uncertainty

"So, you are the nephew of Beru… how interesting, I wonder if he will seek peace to get you back." The Knight smiled. "You are going to be moved shortly, under heavy guard to the Elven Capital, I fear the Queen may be saddened to hear of the demise of her husband to be, and now because of your attack, and the king of Beline's lack of sense in being on the walls, Beline now has no king to rule it." The Knight stood up and walked to the bars. "Rest well, boy, it is a few day's journey to the Queen's court."

Tolm scowled at the Knight as he left the dungeons, he felt the knot of fear heavy in his heart, and he knew he had to escape, but he did not know how.

***

Beru looked over the parchments of reports and maps when Sila burst into the command tent.

"Where is my son?" she asked, her face showing her brother that she already knew the answer. He didn't look up at his sister as he shuffled through another sheaf of parchment.

"Answer me brother! Where is my son?" she grabbed his arm. Beru flew into a rage and threw her to the ground, she rolled painfully onto her back. Laying on the rough ground of the pavilion, her equine legs kickedg in the air as she tried to right herself.

"I am not responsible for his failures." Beru said with a snarl at his sister as she scrambled to her feet

"No, but you promised me his safety, you promised!" she cried, tears forcing their way out of her eyes. Beru looked down on her with unshadowed contempt for her.

"You were a fool, weak. He is a soldier to be used. He has been captured and it is only a matter of time until he will be executed after his torture to discover what he knows," Beru took a goblet of wine and drank deeply before he continued "Fortunately, all the times he was here in my planning meetings, I laid false information before him. Should the little bastard open his mouth, he will tell them the wrong battle plans and they will fall into traps laid by me."

Sila scowled at him as she scrambled to her feet. He turned to her. "You will lead the next phase of the attack, deep into the Iron Kingdom." He said as he pointed to a position on the map which had been under guarded.

"You are heartless, brother, you will not even allow me time to grieve for my child?" Sila said bitterly as she wiped the tears from her face.

Beru rounded on her, anger in his face. "You think I do not mourn him too? He is like a son to me, sister. But this is war, we will mourn him and our other brethren when this war is over and we have our vengeance for the two thousand years of imprisonment that we were forced to endure." He looked hard at his sister, Sila backed away a step, feeling the rage that burned of her volatile brother in waves.

"Yes, brother, you are right, we will mourn when the war is over, and I shall go and prepare to leave as soon as my forces are ready." She said softly, her eyes downcast.

"You will not need to take your forces, there is a new army that awaits you, Trolls, Giants, Orcs and Centaurs returned from the homelands have answered the calls for new recruits, many of these warriors are untried and unseasoned but there are a few veterans from the wars in the other realm, they will serve us well." Beru said as he turned back to his papers.

"Now go, it will take you a few days to reach your troops. Send word to me of your victory, or your replacement will send word of your death." Beru said harshly, ignoring her as she left.

Sila walked slowly through the camp, her mind racing. She had to find her son, her heart ached for him with the love of a mother, and was torn with the duty that she had sworn.

Love won through as she packed her gear into a pack and she left the war camp to head to the east where the Iron Kingdom lay. She passed through to the lower points of the March of the Damned and then when she was clear of her brother's army, she turned due south into Vallonde. Unseen by any eyes, be they friend or foe, she moved southward, away from any inhabited areas, avoiding scouting parties and patrols of soldiers as they moved to the front.

Soon she entered Erellon's borderlands and continued on to the south, hoping that she was not too late to ask for the release of her son, in exchange for her own life.

**

Griffon grunted as Sir Hugh struck with his sword, Griffon barely managing to parry with the heavy, two-handed greatsword.

"Why can't I use my long sword?" he panted, as sweat slicked his brow. The sun shone down on them in the fields below Ellynwold.

Nirimanye had received news of her betrothed's death with the arrival of a prisoner - a young Centaur soldier who claimed to be the nephew of the Centaur King, and Sir Richard and was observing a period of mourning, not that she seemed to mourn the loss of the King of Beline in private, but in public she was suitably forlorn.

"If you want to make Knight next spring, you need to make sure you can handle any weapon, I have had to push you harder than any squire I've had, because you have not had the proper training that your Grandfather would have made you go through." Sir Hugh said as he struck again to be parried by Griffon's weapon

"Another reason why I left, I hated being made to do things when I was younger!" Griffon panted as he turned to swing the sword.

"You should raise your elbow a little more, and not twist so much with your back, Little Squire!" a voice arose from the woods nearby. Griffon and Sir Hugh came on guard, turning towards the sound of the stranger's voice.

"Show yourself, be you friend or foe!" Sir Hugh called to the woods as his eyes scanned the tree line for the speaker.

"I come as a friend, though you may perceive me as a foe. In time I hope that the former will be proven true, provided that your young prisoner from the fort is still alive."

The voice carried on the wind, a strong female voice, with just a slight tremble of hope to it.

"He lives; he is well cared for in the hands of the Elves who treat their prisoners with respect." Sir Hugh assured the hidden person in the woods. "Come peacefully and we will take you to him." He offered.

"Very well." The voice replied and a figure strode out proudly into the sunshine, form the darkness of the forest it appeared to be a woman riding a horse, but as the sunlight shone upon her body, she was revealed to be a Centaur.

Griffon gasped. Muscular and beautiful, The Centaur female stepped slowly towards them. Her equine coat was dappled deep brown and white in the sun. Leather armour covered her human form, her face dirty and her eyes weary from la long journey.

"My lords, I am Sila, Princess of the Royal house of Beru, Sister of King Beru and mother of Prince Tolm, whom you hold as your prisoner." She threw down her pack and scabbarded sword to the ground before Sir Hugh and Griffon. They looked up as she raised her hands. "I offer myself as your prisoner, all I ask is that you release my son, I have information on the war that may interest you." Sir Hugh held his place, blade at the ready, Griffon's stance was less than perfect, showing his surprise and his insecurity with the larger blade.

"We accept your surrender, My Lady, but it is up to the Queen of Erellond to decide your fate and that of your son." Sir Hugh said as he indicated for Griffon to take her pack and weapon.

Sila nodded her assent and allowed Sir Hugh to bind her hands.

"Come, let us take you to see the queen, and your son." He said with a small smile at the Centaur woman before him.

***

Nirimanye watched from her throne as the two Centaurs were reunited, Sila held her son tight against her chest and the young one wrapped his arms around her and apologised for his failures.

"Mother, I'm so sorry I failed you and uncle Beru, is he truly mad?" the young Centaur looked up at his mother. She looked down at her son and caressed her face lovingly.

"Tolm, your uncle is not sound of mind. You have nothing to apologise for. Our people have fought for supremacy for so long that we know nothing else." She sighed as she embraced him again, not willing to let him go. She pulled back and looked over her boy again, wanting to ensure that he was whole and healthy before she continued

"Beru was taught from a young age that we were to inherit the realm that we were banished form, it was our ancestral grandsire that taught him this. I, however received a different lesson from the nurse who raised me, she sought peace, having lost too many mates to the wars that we waged within our prison realm over the years." Sila explained.

"It is peace that I would have you learn and strive toward, despite my own place as a warrior amongst our people. I have often felt the bloodshed unnecessary as a goal to supremacy. Instead I would vie for diplomacy and equality." She said, looking to the Queen upon the throne.

"It is our wish as well, My Lady Sila." Nirimanye said as she stepped down from the throne. Sir Hugh watched as the Elven queen approached the two Centaur, Sila held a protective arm around Tolm as she warily watched the Queen approach.

"What would it take to make peace between us?" she asked.

Sila thought for a moment and then said with certainty.

"The death of my brother."

Chapter Twelve

Sila moved quietly through the forest, Sir Hugh and Griffon rode their horses to a point, having to dismount and leave them behind as they neared a section of thicker forest where the horses were unable to go, yet Sila seemed to have little trouble navigating. They silently approached the outskirts of the war camp.

"My brother thinks I am on the way to the Iron Kingdom front, where he hopes I will lead our new forces to victory." She said softly as she looked out over the large encampment of warriors from the Fae creatures. Goblins, Trolls, Minotaurs, Orcs, Giants, Imps and Centaurs all milled about, working on their weapons or practicing their swordplay, Archers trained with their bows, muscles straining under the heavy loads of their bowstrings before they let the arrows fly into the rotting corpses of fallen enemies that had been tied up for targets.

Griffon swallowed the bile that worked up to his throat. "Sir Hugh," he said softly. "They have slaves…" he whispered, pointing to the group of women who were chained by the Orc's camps. Sir Hugh looked over and frowned, the poor women were bruised and dishevelled, mournful expressions of fear on their faces broke the Knight's heart.

"My brother gives the female slaves we capture to the Orcs for playthings." Sila said softly and with disgust in her voice as they watched one of the Orcish warriors amble up and grab a red-haired woman by the throat, nodding to the slave master that this one was the one he wanted. The slave master unlocked the chain that held her and handed the length to the Orc. He grunted and nodded his thanks and led the sobbing female towards their position, obviously wanting some privacy with the miserable female he towed along behind him.

"Move back…" Sila said softly.

"Can we not save her?" Griffon asked as they shifted back.

"We risk discovery," Sir Hugh said with a shake of his head.

"But…" Griffon started, Sir Hugh put a hand on the squire's shoulder.

"No, I said, we will try to save them later but now, is not the time." Sir Hugh said his voice not above a whisper as the Orc crashed through the forest dragging the sobbing woman behind him.

Griffon watched as the Orc grabbed her and threw her to the ground, she landed heavily on her back with a cry and the orc ripped the last shreds of her torn and battered dress from her body. The huge male Orc knelt down between her legs and prepared himself for his own pleasure. Griffon could not stand it any longer

Sir Hugh watched with open mouth as Griffon drew his sword and moved silently through the trees to stop behind the Orc. He raised his sword silently and struck the Orc in the shoulder, severing the creature's arm.

It roared loudly, setting birds to flight from the trees. The beast turned and snarled at the human, as blood spurted in time to the beat of its' heart. Griffon swung his sword again as the woman screamed out, taking the Orc's head from the shoulders.

Shouts came from the camp as the roar of the Orc had brought the sentries of the camp out to investigate.

"Damn it Griffon, Listen to me next time!" Sir Hugh said as he ran up to them, pulling the woman to her feet.

"Put her upon my back, she cannot run in her condition." Sila said.

"Condition?" Sir Hugh said as they began to move, putting the woman on Sila's back.

"Can you not see? She is with child!" Sila said softly, "An Orcish bastard grows in her belly." She said as the girl was settled on her back.

"Hold tightly to my middle, girl." She said turning to look over her shoulder at the woman who sobbed heavily at the prospect of rescue, the woman tightened her arms around Sila's middle and Sila broke out into a gallop away from the advancing guards and warriors.

"Now, we run!" Sir Hugh said as an arrow shot past his head to sink deeply into a tree.

"Yes, running would be a good idea!" Griffon agreed as they set off at a hard run, back towards their own lines at the border of Erellond. The trees flashed past as they ran, their breath burning in their chests as they tried to escape their pursuers. Sir Hugh looked over his shoulder to see the Centaurs gaining ground, the heavier sounds of the Orcs who also chased them crashed through the forest.

"Keep going, our archers will take them out if they are able!" Sir Hugh said between hard breaths.

Griffon ran over a small section of ground that suddenly went out from under him. He shouted in panic as he fell into a hole-trap that had been covered over with leaves and frail sticks.

"Griffon!" Sir Hugh shouted as he turned to see his squire fall into the ground.

"Run!" Griffon said as he scrambled to his feet in the bottom of the hole. It was too deep for him to scramble out of. "Go, save yourselves!" he said desperately.

"I'm not leaving without you!" Sir Hug said as he took the scabbard from his sword and lowered it to Griffon to grasp.

"Get out of here!" Griffon said slapping away the leather scabbard, "You don't have time for heroics, Sir Hugh, just get the woman to safety!"

Sir Hugh looked forlornly at Griffon, an arrow struck the ground near his foot and he ducked away. "I will come back for you, stay alive!" he promised as he ducked away from the hole to run for his life.

"I'll do my best." Griffon promised, but not sure if he would be able to keep that promise.

The sounds of hard and heavy running passed his little hole on both sides as the enemy continued past. Griffon sank to the ground and sat with his knees drawn up at his chest, resting his back against the wall of the hole he waited for someone to arrive to either kill him or pull his sorry ass out of the hole.

He didn't have to wait long; leaves were kicked down into the hole as his captors arrived.

"Looks like we have a new prisoner, Lord Beru will be so pleased." Smirked one of the Centaurs who looked down at the human in the hole.

"Maybe we should just leave him there." Suggested one of the others.

"We should make this our new latrine, I'm sure a few days of this hole being used as a shitter will make for a fine cell." The Centaurs laughed and a rope ladder was thrown down into the hole.

"Climb up here, human and don't make any foolish moves." The first Centaur said harshly to him

Griffon complied and was grabbed as soon as his head and shoulders cleared the hole. He was struck hard and fell to the ground, only to be picked up again and struck. Each time he got to his feet he was hit with a strong fist until his face had puffed and he struggled to stand on his feet.

"You can crawl back to our camp, scum." His captors said sternly. "King Beru will be more than pleased to speak with you I'm sure."

Griffon got to his hands and knees only to be kicked hard by a strong foreleg, he cried out as he felt his ribs crack. He collapsed to the ground in agony. He struggled to crawl with his captors back to the camp. The enemy soldiers jeered at the pathetic sight of the human squire crawling on hands and knees towards Beru's pavilion.

Griffon entered the darkness of the pavilion with his head down and arms and legs shaking from the effort. He was stopped with a blade against his shoulder. His breaths came hard and pain filled as his body gave out to pain and exhaustion and he collapsed to the ground at Beru's feet.

"What have we here?" he asked as he tapped his blade against Griffon's bruised and swollen cheek.

"A prisoner, My Lord." Said one of the Centaurs that had escorted him to the camp. "He had slain an Orc who had taken a slave into the forest to sport with. He had others with him, but they took the slave and ran. This fool fell into one of the traps we had laid in the forest."

Beru looked up at the Soldier as he spoke and then turned his attention to the wretch that lay curled up on the ground before him.

"How fortunate for us, we lose a slave and end up with a prisoner. I wonder, how much information we can wrest from him, before he dies, or better yet I may keep him alive to serve as a slave." He looked over Griffon's armour. "Oh even better, a Squire of the Knights of Erandia..." he smirked. "Yes, I will definitely make you a slave, you will pay for the crimes of your order against that of my people by serving me."

Griffon coughed and spat a little blood from his mouth.

"Get some chains and a collar for this wretch, then we will interrogate him." Beru said looking up from the squire on the ground. "You will sing like the birds in the trees my friend, and then you will serve me until your dying day" he said with a nasty grin.

***

Nirimanye looked over the soldiers of her war camp as they went about their business, she felt Griffon's absence keenly and fretted for his safety. Their camp was secure.

Sentries were positioned within the forest with orders to retreat should a force of the enemy be seen in the forest. Trackers had marked the location of several traps and the fort nearby was prepared to take any injured troops for healing.

Nirimanye had gone to the fort to see the body of her betrothed, the people of Beline now seemed to look to her for leadership, despite the fact that she had never wed their King, they were leaderless, and she was not sure if she should take up the regency as the Belinese court had asked of her. Would they even listen to her? She was after all, the queen of their enemy… a people they had almost completely destroyed.

She knew of a few young bastard children that the King had sired, perhaps they might make better rulers for Beline than she.

It was a decision for another day for the war had finally stepped up and the lines of battle were stretched across each of the four southern nations at the border of the Orcish lands of Orialas and the Dwarven Iron Kingdom to the east, Vallonde and Erellond's borders with the March of the Damned where much of the Centaur army and its' allies were placed, and Beline and Mithorlas to the west. Much of the northern lands of Erellond were also bordered by Mithorlas, but there was a large mountain range along the lines that was near impossible to cross.

The Kings and Lords who ruled now were fewer than before and Nirimanye worried that their fight for freedom from the Centaur threat would be in vain. Many had been slain, leaving untried princes and young lords in the front. Sir Hugh had sent letters to the princes and young lords offering the services of men of the Knights who had experience in battle and thankfully most had taken him up on the offer.

Sir Hugh came up beside Nirimanye and handed her a cup of broth.

"You have not eaten today, my lady." He said softly. She looked at the Knight who had become her friend. "You miss him I know." He said, not able to keep the worry from his voice.

"As do you, Sir Hugh." She said turning her hand to caress his cheek, it was warmed from the cup. Sir Hugh smiled at the contact.

"There is more to it I think. You love him My Lady." He said softly, taking her hand and kissing the knuckles. Her eyes widened at the revelation.

"Sir Hugh…" she started, and then lowered her head. "He does not notice me. Our paths are far too different to ever be walked together." She said her eyes misting with tears.

"He does notice you, more than you realise. I just think that he has not had the experience of love, Lust yes, all men have that in one form or another, but love for Griffon…" he stopped, trying to think of the words that he needed to say but coming up with nothing.

"He has felt unloved and abandoned, he fears that again from me." Nirimanye said, pausing to sip the warm broth. "He has come a long way from the young angry youth who left Ter's home when I was younger." She sighed. "I don't know if there is a hope for us, I will outlive him, I'm already a hundred years old and, he is by my people's standards…"

"A Toddler." Sir Hugh said with a smile, mirth and sadness shining in his eyes.

"Yes." Nirimanye said, she took another sip of the broth

"Well, we have to rescue him, and then we will see about this matter between you." Sir Hugh promised, placing

162

a hand on her shoulder. Nirimanye smiled and lay her head on the broad armoured shoulder of Sir Hugh.

"Thank you, I just pray that he still lives." She said with hope and fear trembling in her voice.

"We can only pray." Sir Hugh said as he watched Sila trotting with Tolm up to their position.

***

In the Darkness of Beru's tent, Griffon shivered with the pain, his body was a mass of wounds, open and seeping. A slave girl gently wiped the pus from his wounds with warm water.

"Th-th-thank you," he whimpered. The little girl smiled softly.

"You are welcome." She said in a whisper.

Light shone in to the small tent as Beru entered, the girl scampered away from the huge Centaur as he towered over Griffon.

"Let's continue, shall we?" he said as others entered the tent, a Minotaur brought in a hot brazier with irons glowing red with the heat. Griffon eyed it warily,

"No... please..." he whispered, fear finally breaking him. "I'll tell you what you want to know..." Beru smiled as he wrapped his hand in a cloth to protect it from the blistering heat of the iron he grabbed.

"Very well... Let's begin with the battlefront..."

163

Chapter Thirteen

Griffon's face was a mass of agony, blistered and bleeding he trembled with the pain that pulsed through his body with each beat of his heart. Beru kept him on a chain by the Centaur's side as they inspected the soldiers of the Armies of the Darklands. Orcs snarled at the wretch, Minotaurs blew fetid air through their noses at him in contemptuous snorts, flinging mucus to land on bloodied and swollen cheeks as he was led past their ranks. Giants rumbled with wicked laughter and Trolls glared at him with dumb expressions of malice.

"My brothers, I have come across some very interesting information from my newest slave. I bring before you the one who freed us from our millennia of imprisonment. Griffon du Frain, whose ancestor banished the entire Centaur race and its' allies to the other realm, where we fought every day for our right to simply exist, to gain our freedom and return to our homelands!" Beru pulled hard on the chain that led to Griffon's neck, making the injured human stumble behind him. "And we bided our time until the prophecy would come true, when one of their own would betray them and return us to take vengeance!" Beru looked down at Griffon with a curl of his upper lip and a sneer on his face.

"Let us show the Southern Kingdoms that their mistake two thousand years ago was to send us away, instead of embracing us as their rightful rulers!" Beru raised his sword to the uproarious cheer of the gathered armies.

Griffon looked up wearily and stiffened in fright, in his misery he had not even bothered to look to the gathered armies, but now he did and the sight shocked him. There were thousands upon thousands of enemy troops there. A variety of banners fluttered proudly in the wind as swords, halberds, spears and bows were raised in salute of Beru and his quest to take the south

Beru looked down the chain at Griffon,

"Now, you see where your people's fate will lead, and all because you were weak and caved in to torture." He snorted and kicked Griffon's legs out from underneath him. "You are a fool." Beru smiled darkly. He tugged hard on the chain, making it clank as he moved away from the front lines to prepare for the march, forcing Griffon to stumble along behind him

***

Sir Hugh stood with Nirimanye, their heads bent over a large map of Erandia. Coloured stones showed where their armies and their allies armies were placed in waiting for any more incursions into the lands of the South. More stones stood in representation of known enemy forces.

Sir Hugh's face was grim in the firelight, Nirimanye's was in a similar state of stress. They both looked up as Sila entered, with young Tolm not far behind her.

"I have found several groups. Deserters, mostly from the weaker clans of the Centaur host, they have pledged themselves to me, and should my brother fall they will support my claim to the throne, but we must take out the leaders of each of the Centaur clans of we are to survive the battle for peace." She said softly, shifting from one foreleg to the other as she looked over the map and its stone representations of army movements and placement.

"There is a problem though, the clan leaders usually stick to the back of the forces, and my Brother, however, has seen this as a move of cowardice on the part of the clans." She said as she pointed out the different clan positions from her memory and from her scouts' reports.

"The Denaala clan is one of the least favoured, they turned and ran at one of our last battles, Beru took the clan leader and gutted him from his human torso to his equine stomach right in front of the entire clan warriors." Sila said her skin paling a little at the memory. "My brother would normally just simply behead him, but he said that he had dishonoured the entire clan and deserved to be eviscerated instead. It caused a greater fear of my brother to flow through the clans and strengthened their resolve to serve him." She moved around the table.

"I feel that the weaker points here, and here" she said pointing at a place three quarters along the westernmost flank and another at the eastern flank, "Would be the best points to break through and then attack from two sides, maybe even three should we get behind their forces." She said, offering her military strategy.

Sir Hugh nodded, "The obvious weak spot to the middle is a trap, but you have a keen eye there, My Lady Sila. I wasn't sure if this would be a lure, but if your weakened clans are in this vicinity, as your scouts have reported, maybe we could send in an emissary to those troops and offer them sanctuary should they join us."

Sila nodded. "I'll send a couple of my scouts out to the lines under the cover of darkness to speak to the men of those clans, it is dangerous but I think it can be done."

Nirimanye smiled. "I have faith in you, Lady Sila, your help has been invaluable, and we will do everything to ensure peace between our peoples should we win this war."

Sila nodded to the Elven Queen. "It is my wish as well," she placed a hand on Tolm's shoulder and the young Centaur looked up at her. His eyes still had an edge of hardness to them, the boy was still partly under the warlike influences of his uncle, torn between his loyalty to his mother and Beru.

"I would not wish my son to follow the fate of his father." Sila said softly, hugging the young Centaur closer to her. Tolm pushed away.

"I am a warrior, mother, it is my destiny to kill my enemies and eventually give my life on the battlefield." The anger in the boy's eyes was evident as the others in the room watched. "I was captured by these people, bound and brought before the enemy. I have to atone for this in the eyes of my uncle, of my people." Tolm backed away from his mother and fled the tent. Sila turned and quickly ran after him. They galloped through the camp, past startled soldiers as they went about their duties.

Sila chased Tolm as he ran out of the camp and into the forest beyond.

"Tolm stop! You must know the truth" Sila said as she pushed herself harder to catch up with her son. She moved past him and made him stop.

He glared up angrily at his mother his young powerful body shaking with the rage he felt.

"You need to know, I have held this from you for far oo long and I was wrong to do it." She took a deep calming breath before she continued. "Your father's death was in vain. Your uncle Beru sent him out to die." Sila said, the pain of the memories rising to her face. Tolm refused to look at her.

"You're lying!" the young Centaur said.

"By the Gods boy, hear me out and then I'll let you make your own decision!" Sila said softly with exasperation harsh in her voice.

"Your Father was sent with too small a force to try to force our enemies of the other realm to peace, he had convinced your uncle that he could make them see reason and we could finally have a peaceful existence with the creatures of the other realm." She said as she looked down at the boy, who still scowled angrily as he stared off into the forest. She could tell he was listening, he had often asked about his father's glorious death in battle, but Beru had brushed it off telling the young Centaur that he died for his people and that was all that mattered.

"He went to negotiate for peace, but your uncle sent another, larger force without his knowledge to attack the peace talks. Your uncle watched our father and his men be

169

slaughtered by his own people." Sila said softly. "You were just a youngling when this happened, and I've kept it to myself for too long. You deserve to know the madness that your uncle has within him." She sighed and reached out to caress the side of her son's face. He flinched a little at her touch, then leaned into it.

"I want peace because I know that a war based on revenge will lead to darkness." She looked into the burning eyes of the boy. "I want to honour your father's memory, he died in vain and we continued to destroy the other races of that realm, because I too believed that they had betrayed the peace negotiations, your uncle told me that the enemy was seen coming towards our positions with a large force to attack our emissary, your father." She sighed and walked around the young Centaur. "He said he had no choice but to send the force to try to save your father." She wiped a tear from her eyes and looked up into the canopy of leaves above them, trying to force more tears from falling.

"I wish I had seen through his lies, but I was grief stricken, I didn't listen to what I was being told by the mate of one of your father's soldiers, who survived the attack. I will kill him myself for sending you out unprepared for battle, and for lying to us about your father." Sila said softly.

"He has forced me to fight his wars under the pretence of loyalty, but he threatened your life and mine in order to get me to fight for him." She said softly. "I can no longer do this, besides, I am accepted, even grudgingly by the Southerners, the Queen, Nirimanye has been gracious and kind to offer us sanctuary in her lands." She ran a hand along her son's equine back.

"The things that your uncle wants, he has already gotten in the last realm, and it is my understanding that the magic that sent our people to the other realm in the first place has been destroyed, so the only option is to kill Beru." She sighed.

"If we kill my uncle, then the others of our great armies will no longer fight?" he asked.

"Not quite; we must take out the clan leaders closest to him." She said from behind him, she placed a hand on her shoulder.

"I will do it, If I go back to the camp, saying to Uncle that I escaped, I can give them something, poison, or slay them in their sleep..." the boy's body shook with determination.

"I would not ask you to do this, and I will not allow you to do this, the danger to you is too great, and you are all I have left." Sila said her hand clutching at her son's shoulder. Tolm looked at his mother, grim determination in his eyes that reminded her of her long lost mate.

"He has taken my father from me, and I almost lost you, my mother. My people are not what we once were, his fanaticism has caused their souls to sicken, I no longer wish to be one of his soldiers." His shoulders slumped slightly. "I will fight for peace, mother, but I must do something, the honour of my father demands it!" Tolm said with his fists clenched.

Sila nodded, closing her eyes, as tears threatened to trickle down her face. "I know, my son, I know." She held him close to her, pride and fear fighting within her heart.

Tolm pulled away from his mother's embrace. "What must I do, tell me and it will be done." He said as he looked out to the distant fields where his uncle's armies were camped.

"We must plan, my son, you cannot simply walk into your uncle's camp and slaughter the clan chiefs." Sila said to him, hoping her son would see the wisdom.

Tolm thought for a moment. "So be it, let us go and plan." He turned and headed back to the camp, Sila following him, as she watched the proud tilt of his head.

Back within the confines of the tent, Sir Hugh, and Nirminaye looked over the plans that SIla and Tolm had come up with.

"Tolm will return to my brother's camp, he will be able to get in, especially if we stage a chase, he will have some false plans on him to make it seem like he has managed to escape and bring back intelligence to my brother." She said as she leaned on the wooden table, the palms of her hands pressing down on the parchment map. Tolm stood behind her, his eyes taking on a serious shine. Sir Hugh looked at the young Centaur, not nearly grown to be called a man, but willing to risk his uncle's savage retaliation for the betrayal he was about to commit.

"Son, are you sure you want to do this?" he asked Tolm, turning to regard the young man.

172

"I will avenge my father's life and help to bring peace between our people, Knight of Erandia." He said sharply. Nirimanye looked to the young man.

"Tolm, you are an honourable warrior, I thank you for your service, and dedication to ending this war." She said, placing a hand on his shoulder. At her touch Tolm seemed to stand straighter, his body unburdened by his mission, he looked at Nirimanye,

"Thank you, my Lady." He said and bowed his head.

"Go and rest, and prepare yourself, Tolm. Your mother will explain more of what must be done. We will begin the plan after midnight, until then, you need to rest and prepare." Nirimanye said softly, her hand caressing the young Centaur's cheek.

Tolm blushed slightly, "Yes, my Lady." He said as he bowed to her and turned form the pavilion. Sir Hugh looked at the departing boy, once he had gone from their presence, he turned to the Centaur woman who stood before them. He shook his head with a smile.

"That boy would make an excellent squire, and Knight of Erandia, My Lady Sila, should he choose that path, I would welcome him amongst our ranks." He said with admiration for the young Centaur. His mother smiled warmly.

"He has his father's heart, but his uncle's stubbornness." Sila said with a smile on her lips.

Chapter Fourteen.

The sounds of the enemy moving around him caught his hears and woke him, though his slumber was already light and the pain never really stopped. Griffon cracked open one swollen eye to find one of the slave children squeezing out a damp cloth.

"Wha...? He asked softly, his voice cracking with the dryness of his throat. He shifted his leg and heard the clank of a chain, the heaviness in his left leg was explained as he felt the heavy chain and shackle dragging its weight down on his ankle.

The child looked furtively around and then placed a finger to her lips before she moved the cool cloth against his swollen and cracked lips. Griffon closed his eye in relief as the cool water trickled over his lips, dribbling down his chin. He parted his lips and sucked gently on the dirty cloth, taking what water in he could to moisten his dry mouth and throat. Groaning softy with the slight relief that it brought him.

The child smiled softly, "You okay. Mister?" she asked quietly.

Griffon opened his good eye and nodded slowly, trying not to wince with the pain his body was racked with. "I'll be just fine." He said with a rasp to his voice. He reached out and hook the girl's hand. "Thank you for your help. Where am I?" He asked, his face burning with the cuts and damage that had been done to him. Strangely the little girl didn't pull away from him.

"The Centaur king's tent, he says that he is going to keep you alive, wants to keep you around so you can see the world become his." She said, lowering her head and letting some of her dirt streaked blonde hair fall over her face. The girl had an Elvish-like beauty that reminded him of Nirimanye, it made him yearn for her all the more, and fear for her well-being.

"I don't want him to rule the world." She said softly. "He scares me, says when I'm older the Orcs will have me." She hugged her arms around herself. "Orcs took my mama, they hurt her, and I don't want them to take me too." She looked up at Griffon with desperation. "Please, please help us." She begged him.

"I will, but I need to heal, then we will get out of this place and back to our people on the other side of the border." Griffon said as he shifted to his side, feeling the pain shooting up the side of his body.

"Promise?" she asked, looking up her eyes shining with hope in the depths of her dirt-caked face.

"I promise as a squire of the Knights of Erandia, we will get out of here." Griffon said holding his free fist over his heart.

"I trust you," She said, smiling. She leaned over and placed a soft kiss on his cheek. Griffon smiled. "I'll go get you some food." She got up, taking the bowl and cloth with her.

"Wait… What's your name?" Griffon asked her as she stood

"Miranda." The girl replied.

"I'm Griffon." Griffon said smiling. "Miranda?" He called softly t her as she started to move off again.

"Yes, Griffon?" she turned to face him.

"Leave the bowl and cloth?" he asked softly, his eyes on the bowl and the dripping end of the cloth as it hung over the side of the bowl. "So I can wash some of my wounds." Miranda nodded and handed him the bowl and cloth before she darted off to find something soft for him to eat.

**

Beru watched over the men as they trained hard, he kept them working through the day, preparing for battle. Soon they would be ready to charge all fronts at once. Their numbers were superior; he would soon have the last of the royal houses in tatters. The newly crowned Elven Queen would be in chains at his feet as she watched his men strike through the lands, taking slaves and forts as they marched through the lands that they were denied all those thousands of years ago.

Gashur came up beside him and handed him a few pieces of parchment.

"New scouting reports, and your sister is now a week overdue at her posting, we suspect she may have been killed or captured on her way." Gashur said as he observed several orcs feigning attack on a group of Centaurs. Beru nodded calmly, knowing that there was more to the Orc's words than what was said.

"If I discover she has turned on us and gone over to the enemy, then I shall ensure that she is punished accordingly and publicly." He said as he read the last of the reports and crushed the parchment in his hand. "See to it that the troops that are lagging behind are pushed harder, I will have no weak spots in my lines!" He snarled and turned back towards the pavilion.

***

The young Centaur's body trembled with anticipation, he had several bruises on his body, and small cuts and scratches that he had purposely inflicted upon himself, he had thrown himself against the solid trunks of the trees in the forest behind their camp to make himself appear as though he had been tortured, and then rolled over sharp sticks on the ground to cut his skin and horseflesh. He took a few deep breaths and looked behind him. A small group of Dwarves, Humans and Elves waited for him to start. His mother came up beside him and embraced him tightly, he winced a little as her hard embrace stung his wounds a little. Tolm nodded at her whispered words

"Be safe, and remember I love you." She said, placing a kiss on her son's forehead.

"I will mother." Tolm said, taking a deep breath to steel himself. "I'm ready."

He said, turning to the soldiers behind him.

"Good luck, lad." One of the Dwarves said.

"You'll be fine." Another soldier said reassuringly.

"Go and give 'em hell kid!" another smiled.

"Well" Sir Hugh said as he came up beside Tolm. "It looks like this will be the last time we see you for a while. Do me a favour," he said, pressing something into Tolm's hand. "Should you find my Squire, Griffon alive in your uncle's camp, give him this." He looked at Tolm. "Let him know that his place in the Knights is assured, and we await his return." He placed a hand on the bare shoulder of the young Centaur. "As we await yours." He smiled as Tolm looked up at him.

"I will do my best to return." He said his eyes showing his determination.

"Good lad." Sir Hugh said. "Now best get going, and remember your mission!" he smiled and moved away from the boy.

Tolm kicked up his hooves and bolted, the men behind him roaring as they gave a mock chase through the forest towards the enemy lines, they would break from the chase as soon as they were in bow range of the enemy, Tolm would dash through the lines of his uncle's army. Dirt was flung up from his hooves as he raced through the forest, bursting out into the sunshine of the clearing between the forest and the encampment of his uncle's army.

A shout of alarm rose from the enemy sentries as Tolm neared the camp lines. He heard his pursuers lose ground as they turned from the chase as Tolm broke through the lines to the 'safety' of his uncle's troops. His chest and flanks heaved as he slowed down by one of the clan leader's tents.

"I am Prince Tolm, King Beru's nephew, I have escaped capture by the Southerners and have vital information for my uncle, where is he?"

The Centaur looked the lad up and down, "You are injured, Prince Tolm, would you see the healer before you present yourself to your uncle?" the Centaur warrior said as he walked beside the boy.

"Fool, I have vital information to pass to my uncle. The enemy will strike us soon, and we must be ready, the pain I feel only serves me to seek vengeance for the way I was treated by them." He said as he trotted towards the command pavilion in the distance.

"Of course, Prince Tolm. But your uncle is out viewing the troops, he should be back soon." The Centaur soldier said as they passed through the camp, passing Centaurs, Minotaurs, Orcs, imps, goblins and enslaved humans as they bustled about working towards their preparations for a charge. Tolm tried not to let the worry show in his face, keeping it impassive and set in a sight scowl.

The pavilion loomed before them in no time. "I will await my uncle in his command pavilion, inform him that I have returned."

"Of course, Highness." The soldier said as he turned to find the King as Tolm entered the pavilion imperiously.

***

Griffon heard voices outside the royal tent, he shifted the stolen dagger that Miranda had handed to him when she served him his meagre evening repast, under the rough sack bedding he was given to sleep on, into his hand and moved to stand. He would kill Beru today, even if he didn't escape the camp alive, at least he would kill the Centaur king.

He waited until the flap to the pavilion parted and he drew back his arm, his muscles shaking with the strain. he had been harshly abused, and his face contorted in agony and rage. The light from outside blinded him and he struck blindly at the Centaur before him.

Tolm saw the sudden movement and grasped the hand that attacked him. With a grunt he wrestled Griffon to the ground and placed a foreleg on the human's chest.

"Drop it, please!" he begged the man as Griffon fought him. Tolm pressed thumb and forefinger hard into the joint of Griffon's hand causing Griffon to grunt in pain as he dropped the dagger. Griffon grimaced and sighed heavily, the defeat showing in his face as he wept openly, breaking down.

"Shh! Stop crying, Griffon, I'm here to help." Tolm said to Griffon as he helped the human to his feet. "Gods, what have they done…" Tolm said softly, looking over the injuries and scars that Griffon had covering his body. "Who did this?" he asked.

A small child came out from behind a barrel, Miranda peeked out as she spoke softly.

"King Beru did this to him, he beats him and drags him around the camp, parading him as the human who released the Centaurs and their armies from the other realm." She said to Tolm as she looked down at her feet. Tolm put a finger under the girl's chin, lifting her face to him.

"My uncle has done this?" he asked, the girl nodded. "To the man who released us?" another nod from the girl answered Tolm's question. "Has he no sense of gratitude…" the young Centaur said in wonder. He helped Griffon back to his sack bedding.

He turned to the little girl. "Who takes the food to the clan leaders?" he asked the child. She put her hands behind her back and looked down.

"Slaves do, sir." She said softly. "We are given the plates of food to take to the clan leaders and the commanders of each division of King Beru's armies."

"And Beru's food?" Tolm asked the girl.

"He eats the same food as the other clan leaders, but her gets Griffon to taste it first, if within an hour, Griffon hasn't died, King Beru then eats his meal." The girl said.

Tolm nodded. "There is something that I would like you to help me with, I am wanting to end this war, in a peaceful way." The girl's eyes widened as she saw the small bag that Tolm held out. "Tonight, we will give the clan leaders something extra with their meal, but it must be put in after their meal has been served on their plates, the pot that they serve the food from must remain untainted." Tolm said to the girl, his voice barely a whisper.

Miranda looked from him to Griffon who nodded from the sack bedding.

"The poison will take a day to take full effect, but King Beru must not take ill, I will kill him myself." Tolm said as he hefted the small bag. "Can you do this?" he asked Miranda.

The girl nodded. "I can vouch for all the slaves here, sir, we want only to be free and to go home" Miranda said as she looked up earnestly into Tolm's eyes. "If you can help us, we would be eternally grateful sir."

Tolm nodded. "Take it, hide it, and let only those you trust use it on the food that is to go to the clan leaders and the captains of the army." He patted the girl on the shoulder as she ran out of the pavilion.

"Now, for you..." Tolm said as he turned to Griffon, who seemed to shrink into himself slightly as Tolm approached.

"My uncle is a hard creature, I have known this, but to see what he has done to one who released us from our prison and returned us home..." Tolm shook his head. "I have something for you, from Sir Hugh..." he reached into the small bag at his human waist.

"He said that should I find you alive, I was to give you this..." he pulled out a small wrapped object and unwrapped it, showing it to Griffon.

A shining blue badge in the shape of a shield with a silver dagger emblazoned on the face of the shield lay on the scrap of cloth that Tolm held. It was the mark of a Knight or Erandia.

"He said that you are welcomed amongst the ranks of the Knights, and they await your return." Tolm pressed the badge into Griffon's upturned palm. The human looked at the small badge and then looked up at Tolm.

"I will be worthy of this badge one day." He said as he slipped the ornate piece under the sacking. Tolm was about to say something else when his Uncle's voice was heard on the other side of the tent.

"Griffon I'm sorry for what I am about to do…" Tolm said

Griffon nodded and curled into a ball. Tolm pulled back one of his forelegs and kicked Griffon as Beru entered.

"Useless pathetic human…" the young Centaur snarled.

"Ahh, Tolm. I see you have acquainted yourself with Griffon." The Centaur king smiled as Tolm turned. His face fell as he saw the damage his nephew had to his body.

"My boy, what have they done to you?" Beru came over quickly to Tolm, his eyes looking over the bruising and injuries that Tolm had done to himself to try to convince his uncle that he had been mistreated.

"Uncle, I fight to escape my captors, though while imprisoned by the enemy, I was tortured for information. But I did not betray you, I was fortunate to survive, there were far too many and I was knocked out when I got too close to a giant that threw a rock at the enemy in the attack." Tolm said, lowering his eyes in shame. "I killed three of the enemy before I was knocked unconscious."

Beru looked with pride at the boy. "You did well. They held you for a long time, are you sure that you didn't break?" Tolm looked up at Beru.

"On my father's honour and that of my mother, I did not break. I gave them false information instead and they believed it. I managed to ingratiate myself in their inner circle, I was close to the Queen of the Elves herself, and in her weak way she believed I was helping her." Tolm smirked, and Griffon wasn't quite sure if he was being truthful or if he was simply acting a part.

"Good lad, and I was told that you have intelligence to share?" he beamed a smiled and slapped the by on the back when Tolm nodded.

"I do indeed, uncle!" Tolm said eagerly, taking the hastily written scroll from his bag.

"I managed to slip into their command tent in their camp while they were out overseeing the troops train, and I was able to go over their map and write down their plans. I then managed to get to the edge of the camp but a Dwarf saw me and knew that I was trying to escape, so I killed him, but his death cries alerted his brothers and they gave chase" Tolm said as he handed over the scroll to his uncle. He watched as Beru unrolled the scroll and read it, his uncle's eyes lighting up as he looked upon the false plans.

"My boy, you have done very well..." he said his eyes going to the maps that they had laid out, "Very well indeed."

Chapter Fifteen

Sir Hugh sat astride his horse and watched as the armies of the south spread out. The Dwarves

had managed to push the flanks of the enemy to a point where they would not be able to press into the Iron Kingdom. King Urund sat in the saddle of his study mountain pony, his son, Prince Ulak beside him, their battle armour shone with inscriptions of prayers to the Gods of the mountains, the rivers and the forge.

Urund had presented Queen Nirimanye and Sir Hugh with sets of armour from his finest armourers. Nirimanye's bore the crest of her family over her heart and Sir Hugh's held the shield and dagger emblem of the Knights of Erandia over the centre of his chest, crushed sapphire chips that had been set in so tightly that they would never move, shone with the blue of the shield, and a small dagger of silver shone within the middle of the mixture of blue.

Sir Hugh rode with King Urund and Prince Ulak across the front lines of soldiers. Men and elves bearing halberds and spears waited with a mixture of nerves and patience. The older, experienced veterans showed their willingness to wait, where the younger ones showed the fear in their eyes and on their faces, in the twitchiness of their fingers and the shuffling of feet their angst at meeting a brutal enemy showed.

Today would be the day that the Centaur Host would be sent back across the border to the Darklands, back to where they belonged.

Queen Nirimanye rode across from the opposite side of the lines, meeting them in the middle. She looked over the head of her white stallion to see Sila waiting with the archers. Her face grim and worried for the safety of her son. She clenched the bow in her hands as she watched the mass of bodies moving across the battlefield, she searched for the hide of her son, but for the giants and trolls that stood right behind the front lines she could not see him.

Nirimanye rode up to greet Sir Hugh and the Dwarven royals.

"My Lords," she said bowing her head in respect to the Dwarven nobles and to Sir Hugh.

"My Lady." Sir Hugh replied.

"Yer Highness, 'tis a grand morn to make war!" the old Dwarf smiled from the saddle as his pony stamped his hoof, pawing the ground and chomping on the iron bit in his mouth. Sir Hugh nodded his agreement.

"I much prefer to fight in the full light of day, it is much easier than fighting in the rain and mud." Sir Hugh smiled grimly. He looked at Nirimanye who had a faraway look in her eye as it cast over the arriving masses of enemy soldiers. He moved his horse to stand beside her.

"I'm sure he's still alive, Your Highness." He said, placing a gauntleted hand on her shoulder gently. She nodded, closing her eyes for a moment to fight the tears.

"I pray you are right, Sir Hugh." She said as she opened her eyes to look at the Knight who had been a friend and companion for the last six months. She turned her horse away and rode back through the lines towards the bowmen's position where she would take up Valldorn against the enemy.

Sir Hugh looked back out over the enemy.

"Wherever you are, Griffon, I hope you're keeping your head down." He muttered to the wind.

***

Beru held the chain tightly in his fist as he drew back and unleashed the whip on Griffon's back.

"You will learn your place, now crawl on your hands and knees slave!" he said with a snarl as he unleashed the whip against Griffon's bleeding back again. The young man flinched, but didn't whimper. He got to his hands and knees and waited for Beru's next orders. "Keep up or I'll drag your sorry corpse across the lines to take the thrones of the South!" the Centaur King set off at a trot, forcing Griffon to scuttle along on his hands and knees with the Centaur as quickly as he could. Tolm trotting along beside Beru as his Shield bearer.

The armies stood out proudly against the blazing heat of the sun. Shouts and insults were hurled forth from their lines to the Southerners, threats of death and dismemberment, promises of all manner of unsavoury things done to their women folk and their children rattling the younger men on the other side of the battlefield.

Trolls and Giants took up their places to protect the secondary line where the Captains and their commanders stood. Beru, Tolm and Griffon would watch over the battlefield from a slight incline. The Centaurs, Minotaurs, Orcs, Goblins and Imps that made up the majority of their infantry soldiers shifted in waves, feinting charges before seamlessly melting back into solid lines. Beru smiled cruelly as he watched the lines of the enemy shift and move with uncertainty. Older soldiers were trying to keep the nerves of the younger ones at bay.

"Cowards... all of them." He said yanking on the chain. "Look Dog, and see your 'brave' army, how it quails at the true might of the Darklands." Griffon was forced to look up. The swelling on his face had gone down enough that his swollen eyes were able to open enough to just see properly again. His heart beat hard and he tasted bile in his mouth. If Tolm's plan didn't work, they would lose.

Tolm watched impassively, but his mind and heart were in turmoil, he was hoping that the slaves had managed to get enough of the poison into the food of the Clan leaders. It should be starting to take effect now, he looked over to where they stood, at the back of their clan battalions. Not one was wavering or unbalanced where he stood. Tolm gripped his shield and sword until his knuckles turned white against his fists.

"Nervous, son?" Beru said smiling. "No need, there will be plenty of blood spilled today, and plenty of glory for all. The men have been told to capture their leaders and we will make their deaths slow, and for the survivors of their armies to witness." he smiled cruelly.

"It is time." He said as he turned to one of his soldiers who put a war horn to his lips and blew out a clear solid note. An answering roar form the armies of the Darklands resounded across the battlefield as they charged hard towards the armies of the South

Hooves cut tufts of grass from the earth as the Centaurs and Minotaurs galloped towards the humans, dwarves and elves. The very earth beneath their feet trembled with the lumbering steps of giants and trolls who ripped large clods of earth and trees that they passed form their roots and flung them into the lines of the enemy.

**

Griffon watched in horror as the front lines of the Darklands army struck against the shield wall and spear-lines of his people. He felt the chain tighten and he was almost pulled off his hands and knees. He scrambled to his feet and ran beside Beru as he moved with the rear guard alongside Tolm towards the lines where their soldiers were fighting to break through the shield wall.

A shout went up from their lines as a breach was formed in the lines and the Centaur army bled through into the men and Elves of the south like a cancer, hacking and slashing at bodies bearing simple leather armour, men screamed as they fell, blood spurting from severed arteries as they fell, limbs were dismembered, heads lopped to roll amongst the fast shifting feet as arrows fell striking friend and foe as they landed in flesh and ground in equal numbers. Horses screamed as they went down in a flurry of legs, and several noble soldiers were crushed beneath their mounts.

Giants fell to the ground, their bodies thudding hard enough into the dirt to shake the ground and make men and beast stumble in their fights. Many took advantage of their overbalanced and fallen foes.

Before he knew it, Griffon was in the midst of the battle. He flinched as he felt the blades of his own men come near to Beru, only to be cut down by the Centaur King's blade. He was soon covered in blood and gore as Beru battled on.

***

Tolm watched out for the other Centaur clan leaders, he noticed on was not looking well, nor fighting as strongly as he had started. He watched with grim satisfaction as the clan leader fell to the ground as he raised his sword to strike at a Dwarf. The dwarf and several of his fellows promptly overran the fallen Centaur. The clan leader's clansmen noticed and they roared their distress as the fight went out of them.

"Fight you cowards or I'll tear your clan to shreds when I'm done with the Southerners!" Beru shouted, spittle flying from his mouth to fleck at his equine chest and land upon Griffon's upturned face.

***

Griffon turned and saw something glinting in the mud, shining with the blood of a fallen warrior was a great sword, other weapons lay discarded by their slain owners across the battlefield. Tolm moved closer to his uncle and deflected a sword blow aimed at him.

191

"Good lad!" Beru said, as he turned to strike at another soldier who charged him with his horse, knocking Griffon as he went. Griffon felt a sharp pain in his side. He looked down to see a dagger sticking out of him. The pain flared as Beru moved away and dragged him along. Griffon groaned as he got to his feet to follow Beru, Tolm kept the shield at Beru's back, knowing that he could not strike at his uncle until the last Centaur leader had fallen. He did a quick search and saw that most of them were down and Beru's Centaur forces were starting to lose heart as they watched their leaders fall.

**

Sir Hugh withdrew his sword from the chest of a Centaur, while another wretched Centaur was trying to craw, dragging his collapsed equine body. Sir Hugh stepped back as the injured Centaur fell to the ground before he beheaded the enemy soldier. He turned and dodged a mace to the back of his head wielded by a Minotaur. The creature reared back to strike again, a sure death strike for Sir Hugh, but he stumbled and fell to the ground, a handful of arrows trembled in his back and he fell, revealing Sila standing behind him, her bow raised and her hand reaching for another arrow, four archers beside her doing the same

"Marvellous shot, my lady!" Sir Hugh smiled.

"Thank-you, Sir Hugh…" she said, bowing slightly. She felt the wind shift behind her as a blade cut into her hind quarters. She gasped as a human struck her hard with his blade.

"Cease! She is not your enemy." Sir Hugh shouted at the soldier. He ran over to Sila's side and grabbed the sword arm of the soldier before he could strike her again. "Go find another Centaur to kill, this one is on our side!" he snarled in the young soldier's face.

The young man nodded his ill-fitting helmet and ran back to the battle. Sir Hugh looked over the wound, pressing against the open flesh.

"My Lady, it is deep, we need to get you to the healer's tent!"

Sila grimaced at she felt the pain flare through her body. "I must kill my brother..." she said, her voice rasping with pain.

"Not today you aren't, you need to get to the healer..." Sir Hugh said as he pressed the cut flesh together with his gauntleted hand. Two Dwarves came up beside him. "Guard us!" he shouted at the Dwarves who fell in either side of the Centaur and the Man as they moved quickly through the fighters towards the quieter lines where the battlefield medic was set up.

***

Nirimanye drew her bow and fired arrow after arrow into the struggling warriors, she struck her foes with deadly accuracy, watching impassively as they fell around her in various poses as death claimed their bodies. She stepped over the dead and injured.

Centaurs raced towards her to capture her but she struck then down with the sharp arrows that flew with little effort form her ancient weapon clean into their hearts. She felt the magic that had been imbued in the weapon of death. The calm flowed over her and kept her loosing with fluidic motion, each arrow striking its mark. She heard the whispers of Elves long dead who had wielded the bow before her.

"Breathe, Daughter, kiss the fletching's wings and let the little birds of death fly to your enemies…" the ancients whispered to her, *"Wield your birthright, Nirimanye, Daughter of Erellond, Queen of the Elves…"* Nirimanye drew back and released an arrow into the heart of a Giant as it moved its' arm back to strike at the soldiers before it. The creature stumbled backwards and collapsed upon a large group of Centaurs and Orcs who were using the giant as a living shield. The screams and sickening crunching of bones as the dead giant squashed the enemy into the ground was strangely satisfying. Nirimanye ran to re-join the other Elven, human and allied Centaur archers as they continued to push the enemy back towards their lines.

Many Centaurs had fled when their clan leaders fell, Nirimanye smiled grimly, Tolm had done his work well, and she held out hope that the young Centaur was still living, her thoughts went from the young lad to another young man whom she held even dearer in her heart. She felt her body begin to tremble as her fear for Griffon began to rise. She forced it away, not as successfully as she would have liked, for it was still tight in her chest and tears began to trickle silently down her face as she drew her bow again to strike down another Orc warrior as he ran towards her.

***

194

Gashur felt the bite of the barbed arrowhead in his chest. He looked down and snarled, reaching over and breaking it like a brittle twig. The Elven whore before him drew again, tears in her eyes, she had right to fear him, should she survive the battle, he would chain her to his bed in his stronghold and ravage her each night. He felt another arrow embed itself in his shoulder. He looked at the offending arrow and grinned, his yellow fangs shining with streaks of red from his enemy's blood that had trickled down his face.

"Ahh, such grace, such beauty, all will be there waiting for me to ravage when I have you tied down to my bed, you will be my prettiest whore..." he smiled at the Elven woman. She scowled as she drew again striking him in the leg, he stumbled and laughed, looking down at the protruding arrow. "Foolish girl, I love a fighter, it will be satisfying to break you." He snarled as he looked up.

***

Nirimanye eyed his throat, the Orc who had decided that she would be his plaything would not draw another breath. She took a deep breath and shouted across the field, her impeccable hearing had heard his disgusting words and promise to break her.

"I am the Queen of the Elves, what makes you think I would lie with my enemy?" she smiled as she released the taught, drawn bowstring. The arrow sailed through the air, little ripples of air flowed behind it so fast that no mortal eye could see it. With grace that was belied by the speed of the projectile, it parted skin, flesh and vocal chords to slice

195

through the edges of the Orc General's arteries and sever his spine, smashing through vertebrae with a wet crunch.

***

Gashur looked at the Elven woman strangely, he lifted his hands up to the still-shaking arrow and gurgled incoherently, his dark green eyes upon her as she knocked another arrow and held it on him. The world tilted as it grew dark at the edges. Blood flowed through his fingers, his own blood as she stepped above him. He reached out to grab her, he would still have her, but she pulled her foot away from his grasp and shot another arrow, it pierced his armour and struck his heart. Gashur died at the hands of the Queen of the Elves. His final battle, his last stand. His dying breath was a curse on the Elves, on the Dwarves, on the Men and on the Centaur King, Beru.

Chapter Sixteen

Beru turned as he felt the strike on his flank.

"Tolm!" he shouted as he turned to see where the boy was. To his shock his own nephew had struck his uncle, the gash raw, and open on his back, blood flowing freely down his flanks to the churned blood-muddied ground beneath his hooves.

"Traitorous wretch... I will destroy you, your mother will weep over your broken corpse and I will chain her to my throne for bearing such a seditious brat!" he said as he turned on Tolm. He towered over the boy as he raised his sword, Tolm watched in silent awe at the exquisite strength that his uncle showed, as his uncle lowered his sword in a strike, Tolm's instincts kicked in, he raised the shield and took the heavy blow through his arms, sending them to a state of numbness, he fell backwards on his haunches, bringing the shield up to deflect a second blow from his furious uncle.

Griffon saw his opening. With the rage and the hatred he had built up from the week of abuse at the hands of Beru and his men, he found the strength that had been sapped by the wound to his side in his desire to see justice done for the hurt that had been offered to the people of Erandia, and not only himself.

Seeing another weapon on the bloody ground, still in the limp clasp of a Vallonde Halberdier, Griffon reached down and grasped the heavy weapon and swung it, sword-like at Beru. The sharp axe-like blade cut deeply into Beru's human torso, Griffon swiftly pulled the sharp blade out and swung again, striking Beru in his equine shoulder as the Centaur king gasped at the sudden attack. He whirled in a flurry of feet, churning the blood soaked ground to sticking mud.

Griffon pulled the weapon out from Beru's side, satisfied with the amount of blood that began to dribble down the Centaur's hide from the open wound. Griffon felt the strike from Beru after he knew what had happened. He fell deep into the churned mud, dirt and blood inflaming the wound in his side as he tried to get away.

"Traitors, all of you, even your mother, boy…" Beru said with a snarl as he drew his sword back to strike at Griffon.

Griffon flinched and raised his arm weakly to fend off the blow that never came. Instead Beru grunted and fell hard to the ground beside Griffon, who scrambled away from the fallen Centaur. Beru shouted his rage as Tolm kept the bloodied sword in hand. Griffon looked to where he had sliced the upper tendons from his uncle's hind legs. Beru got to his forelegs and dragged his useless hindquarters towards the two. Griffon saw a sword fallen into the mud, blood had saturated his side now and he felt himself weaken.

He gingerly lifted the sword and felt the rush of adrenalin surge through him as around him others fought for their lives, ore concerned with their own fights than that of his and Tolm's battle against the Centaur King.

Beru staggered his way towards them, grip on his sword still solid and the veins in his neck and arms stood out against his blood splattered flesh. Tolm attacked from one side as Griffon struck him again from the other, Tolm's sword bit into his uncle's equine back, as Griffon's sliced through Beru's upper arm, severing the sword-wielding limb.

Beru screamed in agony and anger, a moment later he looked at the bloody stump that once was his arm, then to the severed limb laying uselessly on the ground. He looked at his nephew, "You could have had everything, boy, I saw you as the son I never had..." he coughed as blood dribbled from his mouth from the damage done to Griffons first attack. His front legs trembled and he collapsed, his lower belly sinking into the muddy ground.

"No, uncle..." Tolm said as he kept the sword at his uncle's throat.

"I do not want this, there's no honour in this revenge..." Tolm said softly "Peace is a better way. My father knew that, my mother knows that, which is why she went to the Southerners and begged for a peaceful way to end this, your clan leaders and captains have been poisoned, by my hand, You will die and the people of the south will treat peacefully with us, which is how it should have been."

Anger surged through Beru as he struggled to get back to his feet, "I shall kill the bitch, and you as well, traitor, just like your father... I will drag your corpse to her and watch as she weeps, I will... I will..." he was cut off with a sudden swing of a sword severing his head form his neck as Griffon struck the final blow, and watched with grim satisfaction as Beru's head fell from his body, his face a twisted visage of pure anger and shock mixed perfectly in to complement each other. Griffon and Tolm watched as the head of the Centaur king rolled to the ground. Griffon's head lolled a little before his eyes rolled up into the back of his head and he collapsed onto his back beside the headless corpse of Beru.

Tolm rushed to Griffon's side, gathering the human up in his bloodied arms and carefully placing him over his equine back.

The Centaur prince leaned down and picked up his uncle's head by the long mane of hair on his scalp. "Beru is slain! Throw down your weapons and surrender, we will parley for peace with the southerners!" Tolm shouted to the warriors of the Darklands. Griffon watched as the enemy soldiers turned and dropped their weapons, the shout went through the battlefront like wildfire. A great cheer went up from the Southern Armies as the word was passed like mage-fire and the enemy soldiers surrendered.

The severed head of Beru lead the way, held aloft by the young Centaur Prince, like a gory beacon towards the waiting Queen of the Elves, the bloodied Dwarven King, and the Proxy Master Knight of Erandia. Griffon lay limply across the equine back of Tolm, as the young Centaur carried his gruesome trophy to toss at the feet of the victors.

Tolm twisted his human upper body and helped Griffon to the ground where he sat, his eyes unfocused and his head lolling weakly. Sir Hugh ran to his Squire, calling for other knights of Erandia to help him with his squire, to take him to the healer's tent.

The thunder of hooves was heard over the eerily silent battlefield as a Centaur woman galloped up to the group of leaders.

Sila stopped in time to witness her son offering his sword on bended knee to the Queen of the Elves.

"My Lady, Nirimanye. I, Tolm, Prince of the Centaurs of Mithorlas do request a parley so we might discuss a peaceful end to our conflict." He looked up at Nirimanye.

"I place my life and the lives of all the men here who served my uncle in your merciful hands, My lady." Tolm said as he lowered his head.

Nirimanye stepped forward and placed a hand on the young Centaur's lowered head.

"Rise, friend Tolm, your men will be allowed to return to their lands, they are not to raise arms against the people of the south. We will come to an agreement to a peaceful end to the conflict." She took her hand away from his head and let him rise. She moved so the bloodied boy could go to his mother. Sila looked at her son, no longer a boy but a man, forged in battle against his own flesh and blood. In his eyes shone the pain of what he had witnessed, and borne. She embraced her bloodied and battered son.

The Dwarven king leaned down and picked up the severed head of Beru.

"Let us prepare the dead for honours, even those who were our bitterest enemies shall receive their due honour, lest the gods think us callous." Urund passed the head of Beru to his son. "Find the body of the Centaur King, gather the dead Darklands soldiers and prepare a pyre, then gather our own and do the same." He said to his son.

"It will be done, father." Ulak said with a nod to his father, the stout and bloody dwarf turned to the other soldiers, "Gather the dead, prepare them for the pyre, Honours to them all, no man, nor beast of either side who has gone beyond is to be dishonoured here!" The men began the gruesome task of collecting bodies and severed limbs and heads

***

Griffon had lost all sense of time since he had passed out on the ground beside Beru's headless body.

The young Squire awoke with pain flaring through his entire body. An Elven maid took warm water to his wounds, washing the blood and filth of the battlefield away from his injured and beaten body. He groaned softly and blinked his eyes open. The Elven woman turned and whispered to someone.

Griffon heard footsteps running form his bedside, he closed his eyes again for a moment, and then opened them an hour later to see Sir Hugh and Nirimanye watching him.

"Griffon..." Sir Hugh smiled, placing his hand gently on Griffon's bandaged shoulder.

Griffon began to sit up, "The Slaves... in the camp..." he groaned and lay back down as a wave of dizziness overcame him.

"Sila and Tolm have gone to free them." Nirimanye said softly, as she gently stroked his cheek in unbound affection. He looked at her eyes and saw the beauty in them.

"My Lady..." he said softly. You are so... beautiful." Nirimanye smiled and blushed.

"Hush now." She said, her blush getting redder and hotter.

"If I live to be the age of my Grandfather, and spend the last years of my life in your company, I would be a very happy man to go to my deathbed." He reached up and took the Elven Queen's hand, bringing the knuckles to his lips to kiss it with battered and swollen lips, ignoring the pain for the pleasure of her touch.

"Griffon..." She smiled as tears escaped her eyes. She sat beside him and leaned her lips to touch his bandaged hand. He shifted their hands at the last minute, pulling her down to brush her lips gently with his. Sir Hugh looked on with silent approval.

"Shall I leave you two alone?" he asked, suddenly feeling a little uncomfortable. Nirimanye broke their kiss reluctantly.

"No, it's all right. You have much to discuss, and I will be needed to return to the Capital with my people once the last of the pyres of the Elven soldiers have been burned to ash, their remains will return on the winds to the ancestral lands to go back to the earth to nourish the land and bring new life to the soil." She said as she softly stroked the face of the man she loved.

She arose gracefully from the seat and left the Knight and his squire.

Sir Hugh took her seat; he was still clad in his Dwarven gifted armour.

"Well, Griffon, it has been quite a journey from the gutter to the battlefield. You are a hero my lad, and you have more than earned this." Sir Hugh took the small badge that Griffon had hidden and pinned it to his tunic.

"Griffon du Frain, I, Sir Hugh Aldwyk do proclaim you to be a Knight of Erandia, you have served the people in seeing that justice is done, protected the innocent, and judged the guilty. Your service as a Squire has concluded, and we grant you entry into the knighthood. From this day forth, you are Sir Griffon du Frain, when you have served the Knights for ten years, then you may take on the Grand Master Knight's position that is your blood right." He smiled at Griffon.

"I am proud of you Griffon, all your ancestors will be looking down on you with the pride of the ages." Sir Hugh said softly, tears shining in his eyes.

"You never did tell me the story of the Knights origin." Griffon said hoarsely, the nurse brought over a bowl of broth for him. Sir Hugh took the bowl and spoon and brought it up to the weak man's lips.

"I'm not a baby, Sir Hugh…" Griffon protested.

"Hugh is fine now, you are my equal in rank but not experience." Sir Hugh grinned. "And you are as weak as a day old kitten, you need to eat, rest and get your strength up, so eat your broth like a good little boy and Uncle Hugh will tell you a bedtime story." Sir Hugh chuckled as griffon rolled his eyes in exasperation.

"Long, long ago…" Sir Hugh started. "That's the way the best stories start, by the way." He said conspiratorially with a smile. "There was one land that was divided by hatred. To the north were the Fey, the creatures of the Darklands Centaurs of Mithorlas, Orcs of Orinias Goblins, Giants, Imps and Trolls." He leaned forward and rubbed his hands together, looking over Griffon as he lay back against the pillows. "To the south were the Southern folk, Dwarves, Elves and Men. Now the people of the Darklands decided that they wanted the whole world for themselves, that they were right to take the lives and freedoms of the Southerners, so they invaded the lands to the south and waged war against the people of the south. It seemed all was lost for the southern folk, for once the Armies of the Fey were at the borders, the people knew that there was little to stop them other than their combined armies."

Sir Hugh leaned back in the chair, pulling out a pipe and tobacco. He proceeded to pack the tobacco into his pipe as he continued.

"The Fey were too strong you see, many men were killed on the battlefield. Kings, nobles and commoners alike, the Gods of Death were well satisfied on the last day. Now the Southerners knew that they had little chance against the Fey Armies, so they asked the magicians of the world to fashion a spell, a spell so powerful that it would protect the people from their bitter enemies." Sir Hugh looked over to Griffon and smiled softly, Griffon's eyes were glued to him.

"The last magician to survive the creating of the spell was the one to cast the Fey to the other realm at the pivotal moment when Beru the First was about to strike Aderon, the ancestor of our Lady, Nirimanye. Do you know who the magician was, Griffon?" Sir Hugh asked as he picked up the cooling bowl of Broth and began to feed it to Griffon, spoonful by spoonful, with pipe clenched between his teeth.

"No idea, S- Hugh." Griffon admitted, before he slurped the warm brother between his dried lips.

"He was your great-great-great-great… something Grandfather. He was the one to take the task of creating the Knights of Erandia, he was the first Grand Master Knight of the order. Though it has been said that his magic far outpaced his ability with the sword." Sir Hugh puffed on his pipe and then fed Griffon more of the broth.

"The First grand master Knight was Castillius, the one who sent the Fey to the other realm. For over a thousand years the Knights took on the job of Justice, even for petty squabbles about chickens and eggs we were called to mediate over." Sir Hugh smiled at a memory. He fed Griffon more the of broth, gently wiping the dribbles from the lips of his former squire, now fellow Knight.

"There is much more to it though, we are the ones who brought together the armies, mediate the peace between nations and protect the innocent." Sir Hugh looked at Griffon.

"You did well in your time as a squire Griffon, and you will make an excellent knight. But I'm considering your place amongst us, I'm thinking that perhaps you should spend your first years at the Elven Court, Nirimanye has requested a Knight's representative attend her court." Sir Hugh set the bowl down and looked at him.

"I know your feelings for her, Griffon, there is a spark there, which I believe will, given time, blossom into something beautiful. She loves you, and I am not going to stand in the way of your happiness, you can still serve the Knights and be the consort to your Lady.

Griffon's eyes looked directly at Sir Hugh, surprise glittering in their depths.

"It was that obvious?" he asked quietly.

"Boy the way you looked at her, and the way your cheeks shone red, not to mention the bulge in your pants when you caught her bathing while we were out on the road, I would say you were worse than a lovesick puppy." Griffon flushed with embarrassment.

"I... I have always held something for her, ever since I was younger, she was always there for me. It's hard not to love her." He said from his pillows.

"It is no sin to love, Griffon, I know you've never had luck with women, but this one is true, and she will love you back with all her heart." Sir Hugh put the now empty bowl back on a table.

"All you have to do is love and be faithful to her." Sir Hugh smiled and got up.

"Story time is over, now get some sleep my friend." Sir Hugh said as he put his hand on Griffon's shoulder.

"There's a lot to be done over the next few weeks, I'll take up residence in your Grandfather's house, and start recruiting more squires…" he looked saddened. "We lost a lot of good men in the last battle, and it will take us some time to rebuild." Griffon nodded as he rested.

"Hugh…" He said, stopping his friend and mentor before he left the healer's tent.

"Thank you, for everything." Griffon said with utter gratitude.

"You did a lot of it yourself, Griffon, you just had to work hard and believe in yourself

Griffon watched Sir Hugh as he left, the light of day dimming then returning to its brilliance as he passed through the door.

Epilogue

Nirimanye waited in the grand throne room, her gown trailing slightly upon the floor as she paced. Her nerves were showing as she wrung her hands and whispered the words she was going to say to her guest. Her guards and handmaids waited patiently in the wings should she need them. Her herald tapped the steel tipped staff on the hard marble floors, which once held nothing but a layer of dirt and debris now shone with a brilliance that they had not seen since her father's time.

Nirimanye turned, her face draining of colour. She forced herself to swallow and pushed her nerves aside.

"Your Royal Highness, Sir Griffon du Frain and Sir Hugh Aldwyck, Proxy Grand Master of the Knights of Erandia." Her herald proclaimed as the doors opened and two knights entered, one still wore the Dwarven gifted armour, and the younger man had a noticeable limp, one that he would live with for the rest of his life

Nirimanye smiled warmly at her guests. She took the hands of Sir Hugh and Sir Griffon. "Welcome, Lord Knights, my home is safe, my hearth is warm, and my board is bountiful."

She spread her arms wide and invited them to one of the balconies that overlooked the gardens where her people worked together to bring the beauty back to her ancestral home after years of neglect.

The rebuilding of Erellond was going well, many displaced Elves had returned home upon her ascension to the throne and their realm was thriving. New Kings had been placed on the Thrones of Beline and Vallonde, and King Tolm was returning to Mithorlas to rebuild his realm in peace with a promise to never make war with the south for as long as his line would live.

The Orcs would be the only problem. After the death of Beru, the Orcs had scattered, forming small groups of bandits and raiding parties, which had begun to terrorise the northern borders. More soldiers and Knights from the Southern Kingdoms were being sent out to meet the threat, but their numbers were drained from the war.

Now that the peace had been secured however, Nirimanye was able continue repairing her kingdom. She wanted to ensure that her people were safe.

"Please, sit." She said, formally, ready to get to the business at hand.

There had been several petitions for the Knights to attend disagreements, old feuds had resurfaced with the return of some of the families, and others of noble blood had put forward their cases to ask for the Queen's consideration of their young sons as consorts, those were the ones that worried her the most. She looked up at Griffon, her eyes reflecting the light of the mid-morning sun slightly, softening with the love she felt for him.

He had been so brave, and she had spent her nights beside him in the war camp after they had secured the peace.

Watching him heal, waiting for him to just open his eyes to smile at her, to take her hand and to murmur sweetly to her how he wanted to hold her.

She looked back at Sir Hugh who had been speaking.

"I'm sorry Sir Hugh, I missed that." She said, sheepishly.

"It's all right, My Lady – I mean Your Majesty, I was just saying that we are setting up a school for the squires at Ter's old cottage. The rooms beneath the cellar are ample enough to accommodate both Knights to teach and Squires to learn, but we would ask for your blessing to start recruiting from the Elven population, I know that your people's numbers have waned terribly, and we don't want to take any able bodied men away from their homes to take on the Knighthood unless they, and the crown, are willing." Sir Hugh said as he leaned forward in the chair.

Nirimanye smiled, the rooms below the little cottage were huge, and it had taken her and Griffon a good few days of hard scrubbing, dusting and sweeping to clean them to a satisfactory standard.

"Of course, Sir Hugh, you have my blessing, you are going to be travelling through the lands to seek out possible candidates I take it?" Nirimanye asked, taking a glass of fresh water as one of the handmaidens brought a tray. The young Elven girl offered Sir Hugh and Sir Griffon glasses each and then disappeared back to the castle.

"Yes, Your Majesty, there are calls for us to be in many places, and sadly some of these calls require the Grand

211

Master Knight to attend, but we will be recruiting new Squires as we go." Sir Hugh said grimly before he took a sip of the cool water, "I wish that there was less turmoil after the war, but there is a question of the succession in Beline, the new king may be a bastard, but he is the eldest child of the old king's uncle, and the uncle's legitimate children are contesting the throne, there have been two deaths already and we have been asked to intervene before there is a civil war."

Nirimanye nodded as her eyes flicked form Sir Hugh to Griffon. He looked a little glum.

"When do you leave?" she asked.

"We depart shortly, Your Majesty." Sir Hugh said carefully.

"'We', Sir Hugh?" she asked, not following.

"Sir Griffon will accompany me; I am sorry to take him from his posting here so soon after he has accepted it, but his training was interrupted mainly with the war with the Darklands. Sir Griffon has a strong sense of justice, but unless he has training in the proper courses of justice, then his actions and decisions may not benefit the innocent." Sir High sat up straight as he looked at her, his eyes serious.

"A Knight must not be influenced by money, power or threats, a Knight must rise above the temptations of the flesh when mediating disputes and meting out justice." Sir Hugh sighed. "Over the years, some Knights have succumbed to their baser needs and gone rogue, and it is our place to resolve the problem." He said with a touch of sadness

"Resolve?" Nirimanye asked "How?"

Griffon answered before Sir Hugh could.

"We must kill them; they have broken their bonded oath to the Knights of Erandia." Griffon said softly. Since his return from the grasp of Beru, there were moments he had of dark introspection, this worried the Elven Queen, she wanted the old Griffon back, but she still loved him deeply to accept the changes that had unfurled to make him who he was today.

"I see…" she said nodding slowly.

"Your Majesty, I will take my leave of you to prepare for the journey." Sir Hugh stood and offered a formal bow to Nirimanye. Griffon stood also as if to leave with Sir Hugh.

"I thank you for your visit, my Lords," she said, taking Sir Hugh's hands.

"Sir Griffon, if you would remain a moment?" she said, looking at him. Griffon nodded,

"Of course, Your Majesty." Griffon said bowing slightly. They waited until Sir Hugh had departed and the doors closed.

"Griffon… So formal," Nirimanye started, then paused, trying to think of what to say, she had not told him fully of her true feelings yet. He stood and moved to kneel before her.

"Your Majesty... Nirimanye..., I... I have loved you for a very long time," he spoke softly, taking her hands in his, his fingers scarred and the index finger wasn't quite aligned like the others. He softly caressed her small delicate hands, before he brought them up to his lips and kissed her fingertips.

"I will return to court you, if you will allow it." He said looking up at her, hope shining through the darkness of a beaten soul.

"My Lord, Griffon du Frain, I have watched you grow from a young boy to the man you are today, and I would be honoured should you return to court me." Nirimanye said as she slipped a hand out and brushed aside a stray lock of his hair.

"Then please, accept this as a token of my promise to return to you." Griffon said as he took his Grandfather's Knight's pin and pinned it to her gown, above her heart. Nirimanye smiled.

"Will you be gone long?" she asked as he moved his face towards her.

"Only a few months, I hope." He said, leaning close enough to press the tip of his nose to hers, their foreheads pressed together.

"It will be torture." She whispered, her breath caressing his lips as she spoke.

"Unbearable, but, it will be worth returning to you, my Lady." Griffon said as he closed the gap between them and pressed his lips gently against hers. Nirimanye brought her arms around his broad shoulders and pressed herself against him. His warmth and scent made her tremble and weep with the knowledge that she would not have him back and by her side for months.

They had grown closer in the aftermath, neither one pressing their case to the other, often walking in companionable but sometimes awkward silence through the gardens and the town below the castle as Nirimanye went to help her people to rebuild their homes.

The Elven queen was loved by her people, and they showed their appreciation of her with their loyalty. Many young elves came forward to join the ranks of the Elven army and the royal household guard. Towns were once again home to the people, no longer abandoned and the old Lore Masters had returned to the castle to teach those who had forgotten or never learned the ways of their people.

Nirimanye pressed her lips against his again, her hands trembling as her tears fell.

Her eyes gazed upon his, locking onto them she took a sobbing breath. "Please, return to me, my lord." She whispered softly, her lips touching his one final time before she rose and composed herself.

"I will, my Queen." Griffon said as he kept to his bended knee and watched as she left the balcony. He sighed and got to his feet, before he limped from the balcony and back to the suite of rooms where Sir Hugh waited.

"So, everything went well?" His former mentor asked the young Knight.

"As well as can be expected." Griffon said with a smile. Sir Hugh clapped him on the back.

"Don't worry, son. We will be back before you know it, and I highly doubt that any young suitor will press his hand firmly enough for her to take it from you." Sir Hugh smiled.

Griffon nodded and looked back down the hall to where the Queen's apartments were. At each corner a pair of guards stood, ready to defend their new queen. In the years since their last war with Beline, the people of Erellond had lost much, and they were now getting back on their feet. They were not going to lose their place in the world again.

***

Sun shone down through the overhanging trees as the two Knights of Erandia rode along the dirt roads of Erellond, speaking of the different laws of the different lands. The sounds of their horse's hooves muffled with the layer of dirt. Peace had come to the lands of Erandia, but at a high price.

The Knights would rebuild, alongside the kingdoms that had lost so much, and they would ensure that peace and justice would prevail.

As the two men rode along the road, one of the horses kicked a stone.

It bounced away to the side, skittering down the slight hill to rest against the nude body of a freshly slain elven noble. The noble's murderer looked up to the road, his thick green skin blending in with the foliage as the two knights on horseback rode past.

The Orc barbarian growled softly through bared fangs. If it weren't for those Knights, his clan would be ruling this area and not simply scavenging and raiding small farms and passing nobles. He grunted softly to his fellows, nodding to one to follow and track the riding knights, while they finished their grisly task of removing the last bits of wealth from the Elven noble.

The Orc took his dagger and sliced the ear off the elf, placing it in a bloodied bag at his waist before he roughly turned the elven noble's head and sliced the other ear, adding it as well, his prizes would go to join the other dried ears that were adorning his neck on a piece of string, his trophies of revenge.

He grabbed the elf's hand and tugged the golden rings from limp and bloodied fingers. He heard a noise and looked up, noticing one of his men still held the struggling elven wife of the nobleman tight in his grip, a hand clamped over her mouth to stop her from screaming.

"Hush, sweet one. Your husband was not willing to give up his prizes without a fight. He was a small challenge but a challenge none the less, for that I am pleased."

The Orc grinned maliciously as he moved towards her, her husband's blood dripping from his fingers as he raised them to caress the soft skin of her face.

"And you my dear," he whispered. "Are the best prize of all." He smirked as his men finished taking the

217

jewellery from the Elven lady, her dress torn and her body abused. Hot tears ran down her cheeks to trickle over the hard hand that was held over her mouth.

"Bring her, we go back to camp!" he snarled as he turned and stalked off into the forest, leaving the bloodied corpse of the Elven noble to rot in the forest.

As he marched through the forest, Savrok, the last surviving son of Gashur plotted his vengeance against the Knights of Erandia, it would be a bloody affair, and glorious indeed.

THE END.

www.ingramcontent.com/pod-product-compliance
Lightning Source LLC
Chambersburg PA
CBHW071401100726
47908CB00004B/1063